LOOK MARION,
THE SKY IS FILLED WITH ANGELS

THE ROBIN HOOD MANUSCRIPTS

By

Felix DeTrolio

Thanks Patricia,
And Yes, You Were Right

PROLOGUE

I went to college, as I was supposed to. Since I have conscious memory, I recall being told it was a necessity. In our family, an education was seen as the single greatest asset you could have. I wasn't a particularly good student. I had no great relish for formalized education. I was much better at learning when left on my own. Much happier too. But I did what had to be done and even went one step further – a masters degree, in history. I acquired the degree because I had ambitions about writing historical non-fiction and without a secondary degree – even if you were a stone cold genius – no one in the scholarly world, or the world of publishing, was going to give you much attention. But after graduation the need for immediate income became a necessity and being, as I have said, adverse to academics in the traditional sense, I turned down an offer for an associate professorship at a state college and took a job as a research assistant for a prominent periodical that devoted a good deal of its attention to historical events. It paid fairly well and it afforded me an opportunity to ply my craft of historical research.

My job included the standard two week vacation during the first year of employment, and I took the two weeks to travel to England. I had always wanted to go there, had always felt drawn to the land, the literature and the sprawling history of the place. It was there that I bought the chest, while in London, in a small shop. It was, the owner said, from the sixteenth century. It was in very good condition and the price was right. What could be better for a fledgling writer of history texts than to have a sixteenth century chest in which to store your work. It seemed perfect, as if it was a sign that I was destined to succeed as an historical writer. The owner told me it had arrived just yesterday with two boxes of old papers and he quickly left to haul them out. They were very large, and after dragging them to the middle of the shop, he stood aside as I flipped through a few inches of each of them, hoping of course that they were filled with papers from the period of the desk, which would have been a great find and something worth many nights of scouring. But they were not. It seemed to be mostly personal registers, bank reconciliations and such, dating from perhaps fifty years ago. I quickly abandoned the examination of the papers without taking the time to look any further. I told him I really had no interest in them and he soured a bit. "Why not take them and give them a better look?" I told him I really didn't need a closer look. He pressed me, asking if I were sure about not being interested in them, and I said yes. From the quick inspection I had made, there was no reason to even consider taking them out of the shop. Then I realized he was concerned I might transfer that lack of interest to the chest. I quickly reassured him that I still wanted the chest and he brightened, said that would be fine, and we agreed on a price. He asked me if I would mind grabbing one of the boxes and follow him out to the trash. He hoisted his box up, groaning under the strain and tossed it in. It broke from the weight of the papers and they spilled out over the trash already there. He turned and began to walk back into the shop. "Just toss it in, and we'll finish up our transaction." I hauled the box up and heaved it, it also split open. Then I saw them strewn amongst the papers. They had certainly been in the box, but far below the level I had examined a few minutes ago. Three leather covered objects. They looked like old manuscripts. I leaned over and pulled out the thickest one. It wasn't bound, two age darkened pieces of leather wrapped with cord around pages of what seemed to be parchment. I reached for another one, but before I had dragged it out I heard the voice of the owner, I turned and he was standing in the door. I dropped what was in my hands. Inside we completed our transaction. Then I said jokingly, "No discount for not taking the boxes!" He laughed and said, "No discount, but you can still have them if you want to dig them out!" I laughed and said I might spend a few minutes retrieving some of them if he didn't mind. "Suit yourself."

I took the chest and left via the back door. I waited until I was sure he hadn't been inclined to follow me, and took all three leather bound pieces. I put them in the chest and found a cab back to my hotel room. When I began a detailed examination of them my heart soared. They were in early middle English, which put them from the Norman Conquest and forward, in other words from 1100 AD and later. It was a find! How good a find, I had yet to learn.

It was a Saturday, I flew home on Sunday. I had made a quick examination of several of the sheets and the language was exactly right for the period, but the paper was critical. I had to be sure the paper was period. Especially since what little I had read had been both astounding and frightening. On Monday I asked a colleague at work just how I might go about dating an old manuscript. Of course he suggested language. I told him I had no doubt about the language, then he said "you need to verify that what it's written on is period, and of course the ink. You need to be sure the ink is period." He told me to call Professor Mulligan, at New York University and give his name. I did so and the professor said he could help. He took me to a gentleman who ran a lab specializing in inks and papers. Several days later I had my answer. The sheets that I'd given him (I'd taken two, both of which were somewhat general and gave no indication of what the actual manuscripts were about), were genuine parchment from what he felt was the 12th or 13th century. Almost certainly no later than that. He asked if there were more sheets and I lied and said no. At that point I had no clear idea how I was going to proceed. Had the manuscripts been simply about Robin Hood, I would have gladly collaborated with the proper people to see to it that they became public and let the judgments on their veracity become a part of the academic process. But, it wasn't just another story about

Robin Hood. It was three separate manuscripts, in three different hands. One of them, was significantly larger than any of the others, and one significantly smaller. They all had the eerie ring of authenticity about them and the story they told was so strangely contradictory to the traditional story, that I was reluctant, and eventually determined, not to have them become common knowledge. I had, like so many - young and old – looked to Robin Hood as a hero, a symbol of honor and masculine perfection, incapable of making any kind of mistake. I guess to me Robin Hood was Errol Flynn. I vacillated for a month, telling myself they were a clever and well told fabrication put together by some early teller of tales with a bent toward the sensational. But I really didn't believe that. I thought about destroying them. I came close to doing so, before I realized I was acting out of a foolish and antiquated view of things. Finally I went to an old friend, a teacher whose judgment I trusted implicitly. I told him what I had, showed it to him and left the manuscripts with him. He called me a week later and said I had something which needed to be published. It was, he said, "an incredible and important piece of potential history and it was imperative that it be made available for academic scrutiny, and public awareness." I was still hesitant. We spoke for a long time. In the end, well, you already know what decision I made.

Given how early the English was, they needed to be translated. Professor Mulberry agreed to review my translation.

The original papers, still housed in their old leather covers, are in my chest. They are destined for a museum. I have not yet decided which one. I will do so soon and when that happens I'm sure they will be researched ad nauseum – attacked as fabrications by some, and extolled by others as being contemporaneous to the times and therefore binding as the finally unearthed truth of the Robin Hood legend. Whatever conclusions are arrived at, fought over, and perhaps never finalized, for me they are unique and powerful.

Each of the originals is signed and each of them is separate in the sense that they are individual accounts, but they are a part of the single story and each provides information from the perspective of a different writer involved in the events in a different way – much like the testimony in a court by several witnesses about the same event or events. To make the published narrative coherent and logical I have edited the position of the manuscripts only so far as to place the various accounts in their proper chronological order and have provided the signed name of the author at the beginning of each section. I was forced to leave out small portions that were unreadable due to damage in the largest manuscript. In such cases I have provided editorial notes.

As you read these nearly lost manuscripts, I ask you to bear in mind the old adage that truth is often stranger than fiction.

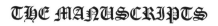

THE MANUSCRIPTS

Cornelius:

As you read this account, you may come to your own conclusions about me, my life, and the persuasion that branded me and brought me to Sherwood Forest and Robin Hood. Judge me any way you will. I'm too old now, have seen too much to care what is said about me and far too tired to run from anyone.

I was a transcriber in Nottingham. I made a good living copying deeds and other documents. I was considered a learned man, and an honest one, and was as welcomed anywhere as any other man. Until they pounced on me as if I was a rabid beast intent on infecting the whole of England. I was gone before I knew where I was going. Running as I'd never run before. Knowing that being caught meant a judgment of the court and the church. And what that judgment would be was predetermined. So off I was, running a mad course to nowhere until I found myself at the edge of the forest. Rest assured, being there, staring at that wall of trees and then entering the darkness of it, was neither planned, nor pleasant.

But, this is not really about me. It's about him, and in a very real way, about England, my England.

My England is the England that began after William the Conqueror, in 1066, had subdued much of the land, and was crowned as her King. During the next ten or so years he brought the remainder of England under his control with the exception of the Welsh and the Scots, who alternately swore allegiance then fought against the Normans, and after much unrest and civil warring and the changing of monarchs, it was the son of Henry the Second whose manner, chivalry, and skill in battle earned him legendary status, and the surname "Lionhearted." He was a popular, but not especially good King for England. He spent all but approximately six months of his reign outside the country, fighting the crusades, and spending time in prison. And during this long absence, his brother, John, ruled England in his place, and finding being a monarch a pleasing way of life, was determined to keep the crown.

It's this time, the time of Richard and John, that was the time of my early years and Robin's, but any similarities ended there. We were from very different social groups. He was born high and the heir to large parcels of land, worked by men of varying degrees of hereditary rights and privileges, who had pledged to honor and serve their feudal lord. I was born poor, but with a father who knew the benefits of being able to read and write and because of that more fortunate than most, until that day when I was discovered to be different, fled the village, and found myself on Cadbury Road with only the clothes that were on my back, a small bag of gold, open fields to my right, and to my left,

Sherwood Forest, large and dense, ancient, and so thickly populated with oaks that there are places where even in the mid-afternoon - when the sun is high - the light is so dim that vision is measured in feet. A palace of trees whose spreading, gnarled branches can be an almost impenetrable canopy. It's not a place where you will find many comforts - but it's a good place to hide. There are those areas of relative sparseness, but they're few. It is criss-crossed by a number of trails and paths, one of which is wide enough and firm enough to be called a road, but without a name. It travels north and south, and travelers and small collections of carts or wagons use this road, and the paths and trails, to shorten the distance of their journey's by going through the woods during the daylight hours, rather than making the long excursion around them, which provides a savings of nearly two to three days travel.

Into this I went. Not because of any preconceived plan. In fact I was reluctant to enter it at all, but being on the open road wasn't comfortable either. There were highwaymen and I had a purse. And meeting anyone connected with the Sheriff could mean questions I didn't want to answer. It seemed, given the options, that it was a good place to lose myself for a while. And my intention was to be there for just a while. The shorter the while the better. Once into it, it didn't take long before my original concerns returned, in fact they increased, and I thought I might have made a serious mistake. Having always lived in a village and having no skills as a woodsman or a hunter, there was nothing of what I was that suggested I could find the means to survive on my own for any length of time.

It was in that frame of mind, on the road through the middle of it, that I met him. He came out of the trees, sword in hand, and demanded my name. I had no weapon and even if I did, I wasn't any sort of warrior. I'm not ashamed to admit I was frightened. I gave up my name immediately, He wanted to know what I was doing in his forest. I found it curious that he called it his forest and told him so. He said "so long as I have the sword and you don't, it's my forest." I agreed with that, he did have the sword and that seemed a good argument in his favor. He asked me my destination. I told him I had none. He seemed unconvinced. He challenged me on it, saying that Sherwood wasn't a place people came for an afternoon walk. I told him I was making my way from one village to another. He pressed me for the names of the villages. I stumbled in the response. He came close, and the sword danced in front of me. I quickly named two neighboring villages, one of which was the one I'd run from. He asked why I was going from one to the other. It was all becoming – as it always does when you lie – too complicated. I thought about telling the truth, but telling the truth – my particular truth - to a sword wielding stranger, on a path in a forest, seemed a little dangerous, so I said nothing. He became quickly impatient with my silence and demanded to know the details about where I was going and why. I decided to try and keep up with the lying and said I'd stolen money. "So, you're not traveling from village to village, you're running from one place to another!" I nodded. "And what's the final destination?" I had none, and that was a problem. I was sure he was going to keep at me for details and I'd make a mess of the story and when that happened he would make use of the sword to get at the truth – which I would have to give him - would feel the same way about me as the church and England did, and then, in that dark place, would have little hesitancy doing both the church and England a favor by providing them with a quick solution. I said I had no final destination, that I was going nowhere with nothing much to help me get there. He pressed me about the stolen money. I tried to put together something that made sense, but it was no use. It came out badly, as I knew it would. I wouldn't have believed it, so why should he. I wished my father hadn't been so strict about the evil of lying. If he hadn't been, I might have been better at it. When I stopped my muttering he nodded several times, leaned on the long sword and looked me up and down. I said nothing. I knew it was all up to him whether I lived or died and truthfully, I'd become suddenly very tired, and very indifferent to everything. It had been a bad day and kept getting worse. I saw few options and very little that was going in my favor. Everything had become just too difficult and it began to seem like the sword might not be so bad an ending to a bad day. Then I thought I saw a smile, or half of one at least. Maybe the hopelessness of my situation, or the lack of credibility amused him. In any case, his manner changed. He seemed much more at ease, less on guard and asked how long I'd been on the road, "And please, tell me the truth!" I told him I left the village in the morning and entered the forest about two hours ago. He asked if I was hungry. I said yes. He said he'd killed a deer just before seeing me and offered me a meal. I was starting to feel better about things. I accepted immediately. I followed him some distance until we came upon the deer in the underbrush. He asked me if I knew how to build a fire. I said yes. He told me to clear a space, get a fire going and he would prepare the meat. An hour later we were roasting venison. He had a skin of ale he said he'd gotten from the same village I'd just run from. It was good. I was very happy to have some. We ate and said very little. I was hungry and he seemed content to let me devour the food. When I sat back from the meat I saw he was grinning. I had made a spectacle of my hunger. He laughingly asked me if I was satisfied with the meal. I said I was. He asked me what I did in the village before I became a thief. I told him I was a transcriber. Then he said it was time I told him the truth about why I was in the forest. My fear returned. Yes, he'd been hospitable, and his manner had become very easy, not at all threatening, but my earlier belief that if he found out my secret he'd make short order of me hadn't changed and his question reaffirmed that he knew I had something to hide. I stammered but said nothing other than to restate the lie. He said he'd been obliging thus far, had fed me, given me ale and now wanted to know the truth. "What's so dark that you can't say it? You must have guessed by now that I'm not here because I was born here! I must be trying to avoid the law the same as you." I said I hadn't come to that conclusion at all. "Well, you should have, because I am. So, what is it you're running from. I know it's not theft." He seemed so genuine, so open that I began to think he might not be the kind of man who would be so quick to run me through.

"No, it's not."

"Then what? Adultery?"

"No, I have no wife."

"Then with someone else's wife?"

"No."

"Come on then, what's left? A perversion?" I shuddered. His eyes narrowed. He went off in another direction. "As a transcriber you read and write." I said yes. "And if you can read and write I suspect it should be easy to find a living."

"Yes, it should be."

"But, for you, maybe not." He looked off for a bit then turned back to me. "You could stay here for a while. Plenty of game. An occasional trip to a village provides the rest, and avoidance of others is assured."

"And what makes you think I need to avoid people?"

"The same thing that makes me sure I need to do the same."

"And what's that?"

"Secrets."

"Yes, secrets and avoidance go together."

"So, we can share secrets, and then for as long as you like, we can share the forest If you're not in any hurry to go anywhere."

There was no doubt in my mind that he was a formidable man, but there was something else, something tentative, almost frightened, like a child lost in a place and not sure why. I thought about it for minute, then decided on a risk.

"If I tell you why I left my village, and you find it goes against your grain more than you can tolerate, would you be willing to simply let me leave?"

"I doubt whatever you'd say would run so much against me that I'd want you to leave, but even if it did, why would you assume I'd do anything but let you leave?" I looked at the sword, he laughed. "I hardly know you. But you seem to be a good sort of man. And I imagine what you've done isn't nearly so bad as you believe it is. Certainly nothing worth this." He patted the hilt. "And even if it is, I'm neither a judge, nor a jury."

"Maybe, but you should know that what it is, is something that made me run for my life."

"Yes, well, I've had a little experience with running for your life. Even good men sometimes have to run for their life."

"But no matter what I tell you, you'd let me leave?"

"Yes, if that's what you want. I already told you that."

"No you didn't, not specifically. You didn't guarantee it. You didn't give me your word."

"All right, you have my word."

I drew a deep breath and said it in one sentence. He laughed. I didn't understand. Then he jumped to his feet. I expected a change to the promise and the unsheathing of the sword.

"Cornelius, I'm here against my will, against my wishes, against everything I've always held important. And so far as England and the church are concerned I'm here for the same reason you're here! Truth or not!" I wasn't sure if what I heard was what he meant. I asked him to repeat it. He did. It was an incredible revelation, an incredible act of fate. I was speechless, and relieved. "So, you're welcome here, in my forest, for as long as you want to stay. And when you leave, all I'll ask is that you keep the secret of my existence here to yourself."

I made the decision instantly. "I'll stay! For how long I don't know, but for now, I'll stay."

"Done!" he exclaimed, "Damn it then, done!" We shook hands on it and it was the start of the most important friendship I have ever known, before or since. We drank more and I told him as much about myself as he cared to know, then I asked about him. He was unhesitating in telling me who he was and why he was in the forest.

He was the first and only child of an Earl. His mother died a year after he was born. His father was a man of powerful, occasionally ostentatious sexuality and two years later, after several affairs, one of which nearly brought him before the Church council, he took a second wife, Goneril. Her first pregnancy aborted in the second month. The next was successful and it was a male child. Robin had a half-brother. Three years his junior.

About being an heir, he was reminded constantly by his father. His responsibilities were a part of his birthright, and it was drummed into his head. And so far as the father was concerned the young man was very well suited to the job. He was handsome, strong, excellent with a bow, had a razor eye and steady hands. Everything the heir should have, nearly. What he didn't have was a social grace, a talent for conversation. He was quiet, contemplative, at times almost reclusive, and with a decided disinterest in the business of politics. Nonetheless he was the first born son and he would inherit his father's lands and title.

From the first he felt no warmth from his step-mother. She was consumed with her own child and accepted his presence only grudgingly. When his father was present, Goneril would take great pains to be kind and considerate, but when he was off to London, or hunting with friends, she ignored him with the same cold indifference. He never said anything to his father because it wasn't his nature to complain, he would simply draw into himself, which was probably a mistake. By the time of his early manhood she'd begun to portray him to his father in a lesser light than her own son. Dwelling on his reticence in social gatherings, his tendency to seek time alone, his apparent lack of serious interest in any of the young ladies who would make for a socially acceptable marriage, while on the other hand, praising the virtues of her own son. To Robin it was annoying, but also senseless. He was the first son and whatever she said made little difference. He was the heir. Perhaps he should have been more cynical, or more perceptive regarding her ambitions, but he wasn't. Part of the reason for his indifference might have been the fact that he was far from the kind of man who believed that being an Earl was one of the great gifts in life. To his misfortune, Goneril believed exactly that, and a stranger visiting the manor and listening to her would have thought that *her* son was the future heir. But of course he wasn't, and this was a great agony for her. Robin stood in her way and she needed a way around him and her solution came only a few days after a marriage had been arranged between himself and a daughter of the Duke of Hertfordshire. It came in the form of a young man – Duncan, the son of a farmer who worked the Earl's fields – who was to be brought before her husband accused of being with a man. Goneril moved quickly and when the young man was questioned by the Earl he not only confessed to the crime but also to being a lover of Robin. The father was shocked, enraged, but ultimately doubtful. The wife encouraged him to believe what Duncan had said, and Robin was brought before them. He denied it.

His father was completely prepared to believe him and Goneril was left with a failed attempt. Two days later Robin was off to London to study the bow with a French master. He would be gone for nearly a month.

A week after arriving in London two men came to take him from London. They said his father was gravely ill. He felt very uncomfortable about them, there was something wrong about their behavior, their attitude toward him, and he'd never seen them anywhere on his father's estate before coming to London. But, they had proof. A note, from his step-mother telling him to accompany the two men home immediately. So he went with them. When he arrived at the castle he found that his father had died the night before. It was then, for the first time, that he began to have suspicions. But it was too late. That night his rooms were entered by the same two men who had taken him from London. They shackled him and dragged him out. He was taken to the lockup. The next morning he was brought before the county officials and those of the church, and accused of perversion. A second man had come forward and confessed to having relations with him. A man named Duncan, a man he'd never seen before. It was less than a week when he was taken from the cell and loaded onto a cart to be transported to Nottingham. What awaited him there was no secret. It was two and half days journey. On the first night they slept at an inn. On the second, without an inn available, they camped at the side of the road. The men who were taking him were sleeping by the fire. He'd been tied to a tree. As on the previous night he was awake, unable to sleep. It was quiet and for the hundredth time he ran it all through his mind, pieces continually falling into place and his hate for Goneril growing with every rehashing of it. Then he heard a rustling in the brush behind him. Then a soft, very soft whisper, and a face next to his, so close he could feel the breath of whoever it was. "It's Duncan. Don't say anything!" He saw the flash of a dagger in the moonlight and the cords binding him to the tree were loose, then those around his legs and arms. "Quietly." The voice said in his ear. "Like a mouse!" They crawled off some distance then Duncan stood up. "Follow me and be quick about it!" They moved a long distance without exchanging words. It wasn't until the sun began to break that Duncan, who was in the lead, stopped and turned. "Ahead is my friend." He pointed and Robin saw what appeared to be a wagon. When they reached it Robin didn't know the man in it.

"Get in." Duncan said, and they were off, over the fields as fast as the horse would move. At times they stopped to rest the horse, then they were on the move again. When the sun had climbed into mid-day Duncan told the man holding the reins to draw up the cart.

"Duncan, what is this?"

"I followed you when they took you out. It was my fault for what happened. I had to try and do something."

"What do you mean your fault?"

"We haven't much time. Cameron and I have to keep moving, they'll be scouring the county for us!"

"Tell me what you meant!"

"Your stepmother, she's the root of it."

"No surprise there. Tell me all of it."

"I can only tell you what I know. The first time I was with Cameron. He managed to get away. Your mother had me brought to her. She said it was torture at least, maybe death. But, if I'd say I'd been with you, she would give me money and see to it that I'd have no trouble. But it didn't work the way she thought it would. The second time it was Cameron and I caught together and brought to her. You were in London. She offered more money if I could get Cameron to say he'd been with you. I'm sorry, very sorry. But we were scared and the money was so much."

"It's all right."

"No, it's not all right. That kind of thing is never all right." He gestured to his friend. "We did an evil thing to you. But I'm sorry. We've tried to make it as right as we can."

"Do you know what really happened to my father?"

"Not for sure, but a kitchen girl at the manor said it was poison. It must be true because now that girl's dead. We have to go, Cameron and I. It won't be long before Goneril knows you're free and that we've turned on her." His breath came in quick, frightened beats.

"Where will you go?"

"I don't know. We don't know. Where is there to go? If we can get far enough away, maybe to the channel, maybe we can cross over to France. Maybe find someplace to live. Some peace!" He jumped into the cart next to Cameron. "We have to go. Here's a bow, and a quiver. A sword. And some money." He tossed the bow and quiver to the ground and handed him the sword and a purse. Robin strapped the sword and slung the bow and quiver over his shoulder, but the purse he tried to give back to Duncan, saying,

"Take this back. You'll need it."

"We have more. We have enough."

"Is this......."

"Yes, it's part of the money she gave me."

"I don't want it!" Robin threw it to the bottom of the cart.

"Don't be stupid! You need it! You're as much in it as we are. You're branded! And she's got all the money now, the power. She won't let you off. She wants you dead! Take it!" He pushed it into Robin's hand. "Best to you always!" Cameron nudged the horse and Robin watched them move away. In minutes they were dots on the horizon.

He spent two nights in the open, following the road until reaching a village, bought food and made his way north, toward Nottingham. Outside the city he stopped. He rambled around the outskirts of the forest. He had intended to return home and confront Goneril. But the truth of it couldn't be denied. There wasn't anything he could say or do that would change what had happened. He had escaped with the help of the very people who had condemned him, and now they were gone. What proof did he have to support what Duncan had told him? He felt a great hatred of Goneril. He wished her dead, or better even, he wished he could find the means to kill her. It was a strange passion for someone normally pragmatic and calm. And there was the inescapable guilt over his father's death. He had to admit to the insanity of returning home to plead his case. His stepmother ruled the estates and controlled the wealth. And money, he'd come to learn, was capable of bending even the best of men. He thought about the wagon rushing off into the distance with Duncan and Cameron, and wished he'd gone with them, at least he'd have had company. The company of two people as much outside the law as he was. He realized that Nottingham held little for him, was in fact, a dangerous place to be. Goneril would like nothing better. He looked at the oaks, stretching as far he could see. He wandered into the undergrowth at the edge of it, hesitated, then moved forward, aimlessly, until he was so far in that the light was dim and the air cool and damp. Days passed. He drank from cold running brooks, ate what berries he could find, took two rabbits, slept on the ground and blamed everyone, everything. On the morning of the fifth day he woke, and as the light beat a small path between the oaks, he decided to take his own life. He told me it was an easy decision. Very easy because he believed there was nothing else left in the world for him. He pushed two large stones together, put the sword firmly between them and was about to throw himself onto it when a deer suddenly rushed through the undergrowth, not twenty feet away. It startled him and he followed it with his eyes. It was a large buck and the way it moved through the density of the trees was amazing. It never lost stride, never lost speed. In his mind he pictured trying to bring it down with a bow and arrow, and knew he could not have done it – impossible to target him between the trees. He sat on the dampness of the undergrowth. He wanted to follow the buck, and promise him that if he ever saw him in a clearing, or head down drinking at a brook he would not kill him. He wanted to tell him that he was his friend, and that they were both tenants of the forest. It was then that he realized that in the forest he was as free as the buck. As unimpeded and without any responsibility or need except to survive. Free from estates and treachery, free from laws and explanations. Just free. And if being free meant being alone then he would be alone. "I made a promise to the forest that so long as I was there I'd treat her with respect. All I asked in return was that she would cloak me, like a lenient wife."

It began there, that day, seemingly by chance, but in retrospect I can see it was more than that, so much more, more than something that was begun with grand plans – those sort of promised accomplishments usually result in foolish self praise and little else. What had begun as the forest of his discontent - entered with anger and bitterness – became that place where he, myself, and the others that eventually came, were able to find a temporary peace. Which is more than most of us can ever lay claim to. And when that peace became broken for whatever reason, even when it became necessary for some to die, it was all accepted as the cost for having the forest as home, and I, for one, accepted that cost as a bargain by any calculation.

****

Our daily life, at first just the two of us, was neither complicated nor regimented. Sunrise brought the morning and morning brought the first sense of light. The fire was always the first concern, then food, then a discussion of what needed to be done - securing game, patrolling the roads for travelers, some of whom would be suitable for the lifting of their purse. Then evening, food, conversation and sleep. I made a journey to the inns on the Cadbury road once or twice a week for ale. And this is what it was for nearly a month before we came across the small party of five men, soldiers of the Sheriff of Nottingham, bringing two men through the forest, chained hand and foot.

From where we were, we supposed they were thieves being brought to the lockup at the Sheriff's manor. There was a strange, helpless look in the eyes of both. As we got closer I noticed one had been branded. A mark that would have been burned into my skin if I'd not made my escape. I whispered to him and he saw it. What happened next simply happened. It was nothing that was said between us, there was no formal declaration about it, and it wasn't motivated by any great calling that we considered our destiny, it was just spontaneous and seemed necessary. We both rose at the same moment. Robin called out to halt. The men were stacked, one in the lead and two on either side of the prisoners. They were taken by surprise and pulled up their horses, more it seemed out of curiosity than because they had been told to do so. Robin moved forward, and at first I thought he had no real plan, no definite intention as to what he was going to do, how far he was going to carry things. But he had his bow loaded and the string at half pull. He wasn't yet the legend he would become. The lead man shouted to "Hold back and put down that bow." I was about ten feet behind him. I had a bow but felt less than a factor in what was happening. I had never been an archer, and it was only during the past weeks that I'd begun to learn how to handle the bow. I was still not very good at it. Robin stood his ground but gave no answer.

The man said again, "Put down the bow or I'll have the hands that hold it!" It was then that Robin first spoke and I think it was then that it all began to change, to become what it had to become.

"You'll have to take it."

The lead man drew out his sword and nudged his horse forward. In an instant he raised the bow and the arrow whistled. It struck the man in the chest, driving home past the thin mail. There was a heavy thud and the face of the man seemed more shocked than frightened, as if he couldn't believe that he had been contradicted by this vagabond. Then he looked down at the arrow, wrapped a gloved hand around it to pull it out and fell from his horse. He hadn't said a word. The men behind him remained fixed, said and did nothing until the man hit the ground. Then they drew their swords. Robin had already fixed another arrow. He warned them to put up their weapons, saying he had no desire to harm any one else. The forward man on the left kicked his horse but made no distance before the arrow drove home and then he also was on the ground. I don't know why I did it, it was certainly not an act of courage or determined resolve, but I raised my bow, took a hesitant aim and fired at the lead man on the right. The arrow hit him in the left arm. It made little distance into it and he quickly pulled it out and threw it down. I felt foolish, worthless. I wasn't even a small help. The man I'd tried to kill was laughing. I reached for my sword and promised myself that if I had to die proving myself, then I'd do it. Robin had a third arrow in his bow and again he told them to put up their swords. It was obvious that in seconds another one of them would be dead and even if the remaining two charged, he would have been able to kill at least one more before they reached us. They must have believed the same thing. They sheathed their swords. Robin called out to me to "Help those two out of the cart!" I pushed the sword into the scabbard, ran to the cart and helped the shackled men get to the ground. "The keys!" Robin yelled. The three men looked at each other and the one I'd tried to kill, who wasn't laughing anymore, pointed to his belt. "Get them!" Robin shouted at me. I was nervous about approaching the man too closely but a look at Robin, with his bow drawn tight and I knew it was safe. I reached up, unbuckled the keys and removed the chains from the two men. Robin told them to drop their sword belts, one did and the other, whom I'd shot at, reached for his sword. The arrow drove home into his right arm, he released the hilt and slumped forward in his saddle. "Take the belts!" Robin shouted and each of us removed the weapons. Then he told them to make an exit while they had the chance and they galloped off, the wounded man bobbing in his saddle from side to side while his companions rode close and tried to keep him mounted. When they were out of sight Robin told us to "grab hold of that cart it could come in handy and let's get out of here."

We dragged the cart into the woods and it was no easy task. The undergrowth in that part of the forest was thick and the trees plentiful. It was fully an hour of tedium before we were at the great clearing. I fell to the ground in exhaustion. Robin said I needed a lot more time in the woods. "No," I said "I need to be at a desk transcribing documents while someone else shoots arrows into soldiers and drags carts in places they shouldn't be dragged!"

The two men were obviously grateful. Robin questioned them about their imprisonment and they seemed reluctant to speak openly about it. He pointed to the mark on the one man and said quietly, "you're welcome here, he," pointing to me, "would have the same mark if he hadn't made it to the forest first." They seemed doubtful, suspicious, as men in their situation would be, but as we talked they relaxed and it became evident that by the strange hand of chance, we had become doubled in numbers.

Lying by the fire that night I considered it all. It was obvious that this was, until this point, nothing anyone had planned. There had been no pre-conceived notion by Robin to spend his life in the forest as the leader of a band of outcasts. He'd come for a number of reasons, and none of them had anything to do with rescuing lost souls. I'd come simply because I was running for my life. And now there were these two, who hadn't come at all, but were merely being transported from one place to another. I asked myself what happens now? What do we do next? And as much as I tried to avoid the answer, it wouldn't go away, because it was a simple answer, a simple truth: there was no place to go, no path back to society, no place other than here. No place in the world outside the woods where we could live as we chose. And if either Robin or I had any lingering doubts about that, these two men were proof. And if I needed even more proof, it was only necessary to recall Duncan and Cameron, running to who knows where in the hope of finding what the forest offered us. It's easy to hide a stolen coin, a stolen pair of shoes in a crowded city, but it's not possible to hide yourself from yourself. The forest seemed the only place, the only choice, the only option, that made sense. I didn't want that to be the case, but it haunts me even now, as having been the only choice.

****

The men were Gregory and Henry. Gregory was a carpenter and Henry a miller. Robin offered them the safety of the camp until such time as they had decided where they would go. At this point there wasn't yet any clear statement that a group of men had banded together to make a life in the forest with Robin as their leader. It was just Robin and I and two men we had, by chance, rescued. But I could see that he had begun to change. I traced it back to when that first arrow had brought down that first soldier. It was nothing obvious, nothing said or even suggested, it was something in the way he went off for short periods of time during the first few days after the rescue. He would go, be gone for an hour or so, then come back, then gone again and back – and it continued for several days. I didn't press him on it. I knew that when he was ready he would say something. Besides, it was his forest.

I talked with the new arrivals and it was obvious they were very happy for a place that offered them the kind of seclusion that only Sherwood could provide. It seemed clear to me that they had no intention of leaving any time soon, perhaps not at all. I suspected Robin sensed this also. If he did, he showed no indication that it bothered him. A week passed and then he said it, at the table we had built, after a meal of venison.

"I'm going to make my life in this forest, and anyone who shares your persuasion and wants to do the same is more than welcome. The only requirement is they pledge that if they ever leave, they won't speak a word about the location of our camp, or how many might be here."

I was struck not so much by the admission that he saw the camp as home, nor that he seemed to be assuming the role of founder and leader, or that it was now officially proclaimed that he had decided to begin a society of the dispossessed with rules monitored by him. All that seemed fair, just, and as it should be. Rather what caught my special attention were the words 'how many'. I believed he had come to the conclusion, maybe the desire, that we would grow in number. I had no problem with this either, but I found it strange because my first impression of him was that he was a reserved man, what you might call reclusive. But here he was, opening up his forest - to who knows how many.

Henry and Gregory spoke of friends who would be happy, they were sure, to come and join us. Friends of the same persuasion. Robin asked me if I had similar friends. I said no, I'd been particularly sensitive of my choices and had been very discreet, maybe even fearful. There was only the man I'd been found with, but I had no idea what had happened to him. I'd made my escape by the skin of my teeth and had no time to look for him.

"Well, if you want to do that now, go ahead, and if he wants to join us he can. But, you have to be very careful regarding who you talk to and what you say. You have to be sure no one follows you here. Anyone who comes here to do us harm, cannot, will not, be allowed to leave." This was said at what we had begun to call the great table. He stressed the importance of the promises we, and everyone who came, would have to make. They were the guarantee of our safety.

"No one will be forced to remain here. They're free to come for as long as they like, but our safety and theirs is the responsibility of all of us. Anyone who treats this lightly, intentionally, or by accident, will be considered an enemy, and dealt with as such."

We all agreed that the things he said were fair and made sense. Gregory and Henry set out the following morning to speak with friends and offer them the opportunity to join us.

So you see it was by chance, not plan, that the men, and the two women, who lived in the forest for those memorable years, began. As many ventures of importance begin – with the need to survive. I have listened for years about what were the reasons for it, and none of them have come close to the mark because the real reason for it came only after it had already begun, as if on its own. I know this because I was there from the beginning.

In a year we had grown to over fifteen. That number would reach forty before it stopped. And all but a few were escaping the condemnation of their personal choice of a companion. Those who were not were Little John, Tuck - the great Tuck, who was the most dangerous man I have ever known – Cally, Marion and Robin. They came to affectionately be known as 'the five'. Each of them arrived in their own way, and no attention was paid to the fact that they were different than the rest of us. Marion was the last of the five, although there was one other who might have made six but he wasn't with us very long. After him it was an unwritten law that the forest doors were closed.

****

By the time we were at the full tally of forty, our way of life was a simple, easy routine.

Albert always rising a full hour before the rest of the camp. The men straggling into the center of the campsite, taking their places at a great oak table we had built. Robin at the head of table, the rest sitting in any random order they chose on any given day. There was – save Robin – no hierarchy. This 'great table' as we called it, was the center of the camp, it grew as the numbers grew until it could seat all of us at the same time. The camp, which in reality was nothing more than a great clearing in the forest, wasn't man made, it was the work of nature and a boon to us. We built a wood and thatched building that contained the weapons and the booty captured on raids and called it the King's Building and there were hut's and lean-to's for sleeping and protection from the rains. There was a large hearth built of bricks hauled with great effort and secrecy to the camp. Many of us, in good weather slept on the forest floor, within the warmth of the great fire which was tended during the night by whomever chose to and even without rules, the fire never faltered and the labor was always fairly split.

Possessions were scant and those we had consisted of little more than what would be called the bare necessities of living. Most of us were little different in appearance than townspeople, there was a good amount of dirt that couldn't be gotten rid of, hair that was mostly matted, heavy with the moisture of the forest. There were odors but none much different than those who lived in cottages. We washed infrequently, both ourselves and our clothes, Most of the garments were made of deer skins, but there were a considerable number of woolen shirts and leggings. Particularly comfortable were woolen shirts and leggings worn under high leather stockings and leather vests in the colder seasons.

No one was watched, no one was ruled, no one was regulated, but no one questioned that ultimately Robin was the leader and no one felt the need to question what he asked of them, and he never flagged in providing what they asked of him. Most matters decided themselves, but when a situation became difficult, or was seen to be extremely important and couldn't be generally agreed on, there was a vote taken and the majority always ruled. Robin never overrode the vote, although if he had I'm sure no one would have said a word.

All members were free to roam the forest as they pleased, but trips outside were carefully regulated. Not so much because of Robin's desire for authority, but rather because there was always the sense that secrecy was the life blood of us all. The only exceptions to this were Little John and Tuck. Little John left every fortnight to be with Martha, and Tuck left whenever the urge moved him. He was the most unsettled of all of us and had a constant need to be shifting about. But with Tuck and John, there was little worry about secrecy. Being what was considered normal, there was no reason for them to be suspected of being a part of the Sherwood outlaws.

And yes, we did raid the travelers of Sherwood. We did this with a sophistication that later came to be used against an enemy that underestimated the generalship of Robin Hood. We had sentinels posted high in the trees at strategic points along the main road and the larger trails. We had long ropes that were used to reach the highest points, then the ropes were pulled up behind us. They were dropped again when changes in the sentinels took place. At dusk, when the last man came down from each of their posts the ropes were hung above the ground on hooks we had driven into the trunks. We hooked them by means of long poles. Because of the number of sentinels posted, we could be made aware of someone minutes after they were seen. We took from the wealthy, the poor we left to themselves unless they were arrogant poor, then we took from them also. The stories that later circulated about taking from the rich to give to the poor were correct in the first half, and only partly correct in the second because we didn't take with the sole intention of providing for the poor. We provided for ourselves first. We believed that we were outcasts who had a right to consider ourselves first because no one else had ever considered us at all. What was put aside for the poor was a specific portion, one fifth, of what we took in total. After the fifth given to the poor, another fifth was sent aside in what Robin called, the future fund. It was stored in an unlocked box in the King's Building. It was the property of all of us. The remaining three-fifths was divided equally, no one received a smaller or larger share, it was the same to everyone, and we were free to do with it as we chose. Some hoarded it, some gave it to relatives, some even to the church.

Daily life was carefree, and communal, but not without problems Most were paired, and most pairs were constant, but among those who did not have a companion and even among some who did, there was the occasional promiscuity, which could cause problems, hard feelings and even confrontations. Robin was always quick to silence anything that might result in serious altercations.

There were those who drank too much, and those who drank too little. And there were the other things, gambling, remarks, threats, all those things that a rugged band of unruly men might consider reasons for fighting. Robin never let anything get out of hand, but he also never interfered unless absolutely necessary. It was up to us to find solutions amongst ourselves. And sometimes those solutions were a little bloody, a little raw, but any fight was always fairly fought and Robin entered as an arbitrator only when absolutely necessary. Only twice did things turn truly ugly. Both times the injuries were serious and nearly fatal. But that was early on, with time, although problems did not go away entirely, they were not so fierce. So far as the two women were concerned, we held them apart and special and they were always treated with grace, respect and kindness. The fact that Robin never had a companion never seemed strange to me and I didn't spend a great deal of time thinking about it. When I did I kept coming to the same conclusion - he seemed above it, or at least uneasy about it. I wondered if it had anything to do with Goneril. Nevertheless, I'm sure if he desired the company he could have had it, especially after Marion arrived.

It was a great sight, during cold winter nights, which were not infrequent, to see the men and Cally and Marion gather near the fire at the center of camp, spreading their blankets on the ground so that it resembled a large quilt, drinking ale and talking while the darting light of the fire pushed its warmth, and illuminated one, then another of the faces. Those nights were and still are, among the great treasures of my life in Sherwood and the source of my best memories.

At this part of the manuscript the pages become nearly illegible, they were damaged by water. A great deal of effort went in to trying to make them legible. We succeeded with about a third. The damaged pages seem to be concerned mostly with a listing of the names of the people who were in the forest, a biographies in varying lengths. I thought it wasn't necessarily in the proper place. If the pages were originally placed as I found them - in the middle - then the water damage should have been top to middle or bottom to top. It was agreed that it was an addendum which was added to the end of the large manuscript by Cornelius as a record of those who were part of the band and over the years wound up in the middle, which would have been an easy shuffling since the pages are not bound. It appears to have been written some time after the other parts of the manuscript on slightly different paper and with slightly differing ink. The hand, however is the writing of Cornelius. From those sections that were salvaged I have extracted those that came through the restoration most coherently. Even so, there are missing words, sentences and paragraphs. Where that occurs they are marked. The remainder of the first manuscript will continue after these damaged segments.

Little John: John Forsythe, his true name, was born in London. Five years before Robin. John's mother was a washer woman, and when that didn't provide enough money, a prostitute. She had no idea who the father was, and cared little about the inconvenience. Her name was Hatty. She raised the boy as best she could. In time, under protection of her son, she walked the streets almost as a princess. Past the thieves, the pickpockets and the murderers, where the forgotten people of London lived and John was known as the giant of the city. When his mother died, he was seventeen years and six feet nine inches tall. He took work as a laborer in a grain warehouse. Two years came and went, working, saving his money like a miser. It's then, as the story goes, that he met Robin Hood, on a small bridge that crossed a creek. Well, that's not true. He met him because of a girl, a street whore that he found beaten and nearly dead in an alley. Like many poor women without a husband she tried to earn her bread by selling herself. When she recovered he found himself attached to her. He told her he was going to Nottingham and if she wanted to travel with him he would help as best he could to set her up in something respectable. She had few other alternatives. She agreed.

On the long journey to Nottingham the girl caught ill and try as he might there was little he could do to help her. By the time they reached the city he had doubts she would survive. He engaged an apothecary and over the upcoming weeks he nursed her back to health. When she was fully recovered he helped her secure work as a washer woman. Then, with what little was left of his savings he set her up in a small cottage just outside the city. She wanted him to live there with her, but he declined. Not out of lack of feeling for her, but because he wasn't ready for a permanent commitment. He took work in a grist mill, he told me the poverty of his youth came back to haunt him.....twice that night he questioned her again about the money. Twice she told him what she'd heard. A week later he left the mill and made his way into the forest........

Illegible here for nearly two pages, incapable of restoration, then spotty for a while, then nearly complete in the last paragraph....

.......the Sheriff's problem. They do John no harm, nor cause him no problem. I should think he would have interest in them only if they made havoc against him, which they....

Tuck: A tall man. Hair to his shoulders but for some reason it never seemed heavy like the rest of us. He takes great pride in it. Much the way Samson did. He wears a narrow mustache, no beard. Strong chin, nearly square, thin nose. Very blue eyes, which can be warm and friendly, or when roused, piercing and penetratingly dangerous. Wiry and well muscled, not thick or bulky. Shoulders wide, waist trim. Among the best to ever wield a broadsword, an instrument of destruction, which in his hands is the most awesome weapon. He is fearless in combat. Some say he has a death wish because of her. Some say he has a death wish because he drinks too much and it's ruined his mind, some say he has it just because he has it. Whatever the reason, there's no one who doesn't know what he can do with a sword, and when roused over a point of honor, he is prepared to do anything, with or without the sword. He is constantly in trouble because of women, who flock to him. He makes little distinction about their married state, but makes great distinction about their beauty.

Regarding his title 'Friar', it's not as the legend has it. He was never ordained, and certainly, as some say, defrocked. The title was gratuitously given to him by the monks who raised him – he was orphaned and brought to the monastery while still an infant. He wore the robes while he was young, but once he left, which he did against the counseling of the friars, he doesn't wear them at all, except on holy days and then out of respect for the men who raised him. When he has them on, he is proud to announce, "I avoid beds, drink, and other pleasures."

He is respected as a man of his word, so long as that word is not given to a woman, for a woman, about a woman. The only exception, is "that woman." To her he gave his word and never broke it. Very few know the name and those who do know it never speak it. Some out of respect for

Tuck, and some out of fear – he's said more than once that he doesn't want to hear it, ever.

Here there are lines that cannot be read, and there are several attempts by the author to scratch out what had been written. This is the only place in the entire first manuscript where such a thing occurs. The violence of the lines is such that the pen penetrated the paper. Something very dramatic must have induced the writer to decide that those lines should never be read. It begins again with the following, which has several unreadable sections marked by us with the customary dots.

Robin calls him Tuck the terrible....his entrance to us.... They're great friends. He came to the group not long after Little John....like John he is....persuasion......quick to laugh, and just as quick to temper. He leaves when he chooses, mostly when he wants a woman. He always returns drunk. It's a long time now that he's been gone, so once, just once, I say the name not to be said. And as I say it I'll write it down because I believe it should be known. She is also long gone, long ago left the lands of her husband's estate in Kent. I call her back now. I call her Cicely.

Alan-a-dale: Short, stocky and with a great deep laugh. Happy all the time.....he...... his companion were always......his skill at music was agreed to be the best and most perfected anyone of us had heard. He played his flute almost every night around the fire. He wasn't much with the bow but he had plenty of courage......wounded once and......his companion died in the great battle outside the forest, he never had another, and his songs became......I miss the sound of his flute, it was in perfect harmony with the forest. I believe, if he had been different, socially acceptable he might have made a name for himself with that flute.

Will Scarlett: Named for the deep color of his hood. Robin called him the red bird and said that he could be spotted for miles, which wasn't quite true because whenever we were outside the camp he turned the hood down. He was of an eagles eye and was always up the trees looking ….the great battle he was......not long before the raid by Thoren he brought Archibald into camp.

Archie: A great sense of humor, and always the first to see the comedy in the tragedy. I think he did that because in reality he was, like most clowns, a sad man. He was the one who made the majority of the trips into the villages to get the ale and whatever else the forest didn't provide. He took Guthrie with him most of the time. They were companions the whole time I was in the forest. Guthrie was very good with a bow.

Gregory: He had a great head for numbers and so he was the one who made the tallies, did the calculations for dividing up the gold and whatever else we took. You could trust him without reserve when it came to the money, or anything else for that matter. He seemed to have a fanatic need to never make a mistake with numbers and just as fanatical a need to be honest about everything else. Sometimes, when that honesty was verbal and about someone, it could be offensive, but I don't think he ever meant it that way. He just couldn't be any other way. I liked him very much. Most of us did.

Wayne: He was the companion of Jonathan and he never fought, never was sentinel, never was a party to the taking of a purse. He simply couldn't do any of it. He believed in things that were sometimes a little strange, but was so good-hearted that we all accepted him, and because he wouldn't fight there wasn't a man in the camp who would not have protected him with their life.

Here we begin again with the body of the first manuscript, that of Cornelius.

****

The great battle, as it came to be called was fought in the early Spring of my third year in the forest. Up to that point we had earned a reputation as a band of perverted evaders of justice. We were called outlaws, but the truth is that outlaws, thieves hiding in a forest, would have been looked on with less disgust than we were. To call us outlaws was said to be a compliment. We cared little for whatever they called us. The forest had become our home, we knew it like no one else. By the spring of the second year we were forty in number. With only two women, thirty seven armed men capable of fighting and one who would not kill. Not such a great number in comparison to what the Sheriff of Nottingham could have mounted against us, but we had the forest and while inside it were, for all practical purposes, impregnable. The outposts that surrounded our campsite stretched in every direction for long distances, manned by the best of our archers who were, as I said before, posted high in the trees where they were nearly invulnerable. We had mapped a great deal of the landscape and our communications between the sentinels and the camp was excellent and quick. We took virtually what we wanted when we wanted from anyone who traveled the forest, and although traffic through Sherwood had diminished since we became inhabitants, there was still a notable flow of wagons, travelers and caravans. The reason for this was that at least two days, frequently more, was lost by going around Sherwood and there were the bandits who pillaged the main roads which made them only a little less dangerous than the forest roads.

The battle which marked a turning point in our fragile existence took place in the early spring and came about because of what Tuck had learned while in Nottingham. This is how it happened.

Robin, tossing the purse in the air. "And where did you get this?"

Tuck said he had sources. "People who understand the work I do, and the value of it." Little John said "if it's work that got you that purse, then you must have gotten it lying down." Robin tossed the purse to me. I opened it and poured the contents onto the table. Six pounds and one shilling. Robin said she must be wealthy. Tuck said she wasn't poor. Then he said he had more than just the purse.

What he had was information about a caravan, escorted by the Sheriff's men that would pass on the West road just at the edge of the forest. The numbers he told about the gold and silver were extraordinary. It fired the imagination of the men. Robin wondered about the source of it. Tuck said he was told it was tax money from Nottingham being sent to Prince John and the veracity of it was beyond question – the information had come from the same place as the purse. The reference to Prince John cooled the imaginations quickly. Harassing the wealthy who passed through, even ambushing a moderate shipment of the Sheriff, though dangerous and certain to give the Sheriff fits, was nothing in comparison to waylaying taxes to the Prince.

There was an ominous feeling about such a venture, no matter what the booty. It was discussed in general and in small groups for several days before Robin called a meeting two weeks before the day the gold would be passing through Sherwood. A decision had to be made one way or the other. Some were for it. Some against it. A vote was called. The spilt was even. The meeting ended without a decision. Two days passed and it seemed that the topic wasn't to be forgotten. It was a constant source of controversy at night before the fire. And some of those who were against it at the outset had become convinced it should be done. Another meeting was called. Robin said,

"We can talk through the night if necessary, but before the sun's up, we'll end with a vote and that vote is final. It's too near the date to say no today and yes two days from now. Even if we decide a yes tonight, we'll be hard pressed to be ready. Bear in mind the fight must be made outside the forest. We've never done that. It'll be risky at best. Do your talking, and then we vote. If it's yes, there's a lot to do, and quickly, if no, it's over. We'll hear no more of it."

The talk went on late into the night, the fire roared as did the opinions. The women, who sat silent at the far end of the camp looked unusually ill at ease. And the reasons were obvious to everyone. At best many would not return from such an engagement.

Was it necessary at all? Even to this day I have no single feeling about it. Having such great sums would be fine and good and might afford us options we had never had before. Maybe even the opportunity to find a way to the continent where it was rumored that in certain cities in France people such as us, although not openly welcome, would be ignored – so long as we kept to our own kind. If that were true, having the means to go there would be the best of things. If false then the risk to get the gold had less to recommend it, and given the Church's decree that only hell awaited us in death, avoiding that possibility by ignoring the gold and remaining in the forest seemed a less risky alternative. With the moon high a vote was finally called. For myself, never having gotten the full sense of being a warrior, it was a testy business at best. I'd rather been able to supply us with gold by the power of my pen, but that was impossible. I was against it, but like everyone else, if it passed I'd put my life on it. So, we voted. It passed by a slim majority. Tuck voted yes and so did Little John. Because the women didn't vote thirty-eight ballots would be cast, which could have resulted in a stalemate, so, to avoid that possibility, Robin didn't vote. It seemed to me, who had been with him the longest, that although he'd not said a word in favor or against it, he was well concerned about the losses that were inevitable. After the vote most went to sleep. I was awake. Robin motioned to me and we walked the perimeter of the camp.

He asked me what I thought of it. The going out and exposing ourselves to mounted troops. "Pen, what do you think of it?" He'd been calling me Pen for some time. He said Cornelius was too stiff a name and in deference to the fact that I'd earned my living with the pen he thought it an appropriate substitution. I told him being out of the forest seemed dangerous to me. The forest was our best weapon. And we were not going to be taking purses from travelers who were frightened out of their wits, we were going into war without our best weapon. Of course it seemed dangerous. And he was concerned that it was the Prince's gold. And it would without doubt call more attention to us than anything we had done thus far. I was in agreement with that. For my part I was more concerned about the attention than anything else. We had been successful doing things the way we had been doing them. We created some angry merchants, some lower ranking land owners, but we had never taken anything that belonged directly to the Sheriff or the Prince. I told him he could have called it off. He said, "We voted." But no one would have contradicted him. He laughed and said that he wasn't Caesar. I said that to us, he was and he said that whether that was true or not, once you overrule the majority "what's to stop you from doing it again, just to please your own fancy?" "Nothing I guess, except your character." He laughed again and said he had first hand knowledge about how power can have a strange influence over character. I couldn't disagree with that. Then he said, "It's a lot of gold." Yes, if it was what we were told it was, it was a lot of gold.

****

It's a big forest and we had rambled over all of it, knowing it like you would know the rooms of your house. We were well organized, archers, ground men, makers of clothing, and keepers of the camp. Sweeping down from the trees, appearing from the underbrush as if we came out of nowhere and then disappearing into the density of it all. Camouflage and deception had been the staple of our success. Now we would abandon the safety of the oaks to fight on open ground. It was impossible not to be worried about it. Our greatest source of comfort was that we knew Robin would plan it well. He stressed the need for the archers to do deep damage with the first two volleys. He felt this was the key to everything. If the enemy could be heavily damaged, then attacked, then in the heat of battle we made a false retreat and lured them into the first of the trees and the underbrush, we might win the day without heavy losses. He traveled the road the caravan would take every day for a week until he was satisfied that he had found the most advantageous place - where the trees were very thick and the archers could strike from high up, doing as much damage as possible while we still had surprise as our ally.

The morning of the battle I was with Little John when he woke Robin, who was sleeping on his deerskin some way out from the clearing where the rest of us had kept warm by the great fire. When something was strongly on his mind he would do this – sleep out of the clearing in a solitary communion with the woods. He was a light sleeper and was on his feet at the first distant sound of our footsteps. He could hear the footsteps long before he could see us because the morning fog was heavy. He had his leggings on while we were still twenty feet from him. By the time we reached him he was at the ready, shouldering his bow and quiver. John told him it was "A long column, heading in the direction of Shockwell. They'll move west from there." Robin nodded and we moved toward the camp.

Albert was true to his early morning ritual and had pots blazing over the fire. There are seven men in the clearing, six of whom will stay behind and guard the campsite. Cally was assisting Albert. Marion was finishing Jonathan's quiver. Wayne stood close to Jonathan. When Marion finished putting in the last arrow Jonathan slung the quiver over his shoulder, went to Wayne and they talked quietly. Wayne had no weapons, he was never a part of the attack. He was the one I mentioned earlier who would not kill. The taking of a life, whatever the reason, was impossible for him. He said it was a communion with an eternal truth. He said things like that often. The men called them 'large word things.' It was said jokingly that I had taught him to use big words so that he would sound important. There were those of us who thought we understood why he felt the way he did, and those who didn't, and those who didn't care one way or the other. Several said he should have been a monk, or a transcriber like myself. But in the end he was accepted for what he was and no one held it against him that he didn't fight. I could see that Wayne wasn't happy. But neither was I, nor anyone who was about to move out. I'm sure Jonathan would have rather not had to go, he'd voted against it, but he knew it had to be done and I could see he was getting impatient. He saw us coming out of the woods and I knew he wanted help. I shouted out to him and waved him over, he nodded, held Wayne for a second, then was into the forest with us. Wayne called after him to be careful. Jonathan reached us laughing, and said Wayne worries too much. I agreed, but what I really felt was that Wayne was right. Today was something to worry about. I remember telling myself that there was nothing fine about war and killing, whatever the reason for it. I wished Tuck were with us, but two days ago he'd fallen down a slope and broken his ankle. He was in Shockwell being attended to by the monks. Having Tuck and his broadsword was like having five extra men. It was a full two hours walk to the place Robin had selected.

****

I heard Scarlett call out from his perch in the oaks, "I can see the dust from horses." Robin asked how far and Will said about five miles but that it was too soon to be sure. Robin shouted back, "Do we have half an hour?" And Will said that half an hour seemed safe. Robin asked Little John if everyone was in place and John said they were, Robin told him to re-check the north side of the line and for me to check the south side. I did and came back and told him everything was ready, John did the same and then he signaled Scarlett, and we took our places with the men on the ground. Robin began to walk the line at the forest edge, giving words of encouragement and pats on the back. As he moved through the undergrowth, I could hear his feet crushing dried twigs and parched leaves, it was different than in the forest where the moisture made your steps softer, quieter, easier to conceal. And there was much more light falling on him. And his leggings had lost the glisten the dampness always gave them. They were dry and brightly brown. I looked at my own and they were the same. We were not home. We were at the edge of their world and things were different. I hoped we were not making a very big mistake. I heard Robin call out to Calvin about the archers being ready. He answered yes. It sounded like his voice was falling through the branches. He and his men were well hidden in the leaves and the trunks of the oaks. I knew Robin was concerned, he kept moving up and down the row, then he stopped and looked back to Calvin. He gave him a final warning, saying that there could be no mistakes, they must be accurate, anything less would mean a nearly impossible situation for the men on the ground. "Open ground! We'll be out on open ground! You have to be accurate!" I knew how important those men in the trees were to us. If they took a great number with the first volley we would not only have surprise as our ally, but also confusion and some fear. An accurate second volley as we moved out of the woods would go a long way to having us carry the day. I could see the same hope and the same concern on the faces of the men. This was the first time we were going to be fighting in the open, without the oaks to hide us. Less than accuracy and there most certainly would be disaster. That was the fact we all lived with while we waited. Calvin assured Robin they would be accurate, and fast. Robin moved down the line toward John, "It's nearly time." He told him. John was ready, we all were - then, in a whisper that I could just hear, "This may be costly John," and John's reply, "We'll be fine. We have surprise. They'll never expect us to strike in the open." Robin smiled and told him he was depending on that. It was a weak smile, the kind you see when someone is trying to make light of something and not quite able to do so. I saw Robin bite on his lip, it was something he did often, almost unconsciously I think. He nodded to me, told me to be ready. I was. Then he began a

quick walk from the line, about five yards toward
the edge of the woods, a straight line that took
him into the low growing thicket that separates
the forest from the open land, and then out into
the clearing. The light beyond the edge of the
woods was bright, intense, yellow white. My eyes
followed the same line and saw, just at the edge
of vision, the summer castle of Prince John, on a
tall hill. The distance was nearly two miles. The
castle shimmered and vibrated in the warm air. I
thought how nice it must be to live in a place like
that, with servants and all the food you could eat.
The castle was empty now, but would be filled
when the weather warmed. Then it was John
saying, "Robin! Will just came down. They're
only half a mile." I tensed up quickly, so did the
others, I could see them gripping the sword hilts
so tightly that their veins stood up like ropes.
"Check the line again!" Robin was back into the
trees. Surprise seemed assured. I felt good about
that. We badly needed surprise. It was the best
thing to have, except for Tuck and Little John.
But we had only one of them, and nothing could
substitute for the second, even surprise. He would
have been a great help. Robin called out to John
who had moved far down the line telling
everyone to be ready, be strong. "After the
archers, we move into the open, on my signal. It
must be quick. We have to be on them before
they can turn on us." I remember those words, the
sense of control in them. Robin always gave you
the feeling that in the end, whether he had doubts

or not, he would take you home safely. John ran quickly back to him and I heard him ask about a retreat if it went badly. "If it goes badly, I'll sound it, if I do, get them back into the woods, far back, if they follow, use the trees to make a fight of it. The horses won't be much help to them in the woods. Don't let them be hacked."

I looked to the clearing, the horses of the caravan could be seen. It would be soon and with the nearness of it, the silence became more than before. And very tense. You could feel it in the air. All my senses seemed to come alive as they had never been before, all pulling at me at the same time. I heard a mouse running over the carpet of leaves, a small grey one that stopped to wiggle his nose and wonder what we were all doing here, I saw a spider silently crawling on my sleeve, a trail of ants was mounting a mound just to the right of me, a bird dropping fell into the leaves, then the mouse climbed over my foot. I had not noticed much of anything before, and now I was seeing everything, in vivid colors and hearing everything in hard, solid sounds. And it was all happening at once. Then I thought I heard the sound of thunder, but it was my blood pounding in my ears. I heard the distant beat of horses hoofs on the ground getting very close. I felt the earth shaking. Everything was ten times what it was. I looked around, everyone was poised, rigid, hard. And then there was the slow pass of the enemy in front of us. I waited to hear the archers release and there was that very long, slow second, a moment that seems to never end. I wondered why I was there, I was sure the others felt the same way, they had too. I wondered if there was another way, another choice – what would happen if the command were never given and no one was asked to die.

I saw Robin raise his arm, then lower it. Then it all began to happen very fast. The air was broken by the whistle of arrows, I watched them plunge downward at the targets. The soldiers of the Sheriff's caravan pulled up their horses, the sound wasn't unfamiliar to them. They turned their heads to the tree tops, they knew what would be coming down. The first barrage was accurate. The sounds changed from whistling arrows, to arrows hitting steel, flesh, - solid, heavy thumping, sounds. We were shouted to our feet. The second volley was less deadly, but effective and we were out of the woods and on them. Then the wildness began. Horses were rearing in panic and were just as dangerous with their hoofs as were the swords of the Sheriff's men. The wounded tried to hold their saddle, blood poured from open wounds and dripped to the ground like a soft red rain. I lashed out at them, able to hit only legs and occasionally an arm because the horses held them above us. All of it was closely held and that was good for us and bad for them. They were caught in a tight space and even though they struck down at us, I sensed that being mounted wasn't to their advantage. The horses stomped and twisted and kept them constantly off balance while we hacked at them. When a man fell from his horse he was finished - we railed at those on the ground and their armor was a prison and a death sentence. I caught glimpses of Robin in and out of the tangle of horses, slashing with his sword. Little John towered above everyone and was the only man who could fight the horsemen as if they were on even ground. He moved like death incarnate among them, cutting them down like a reaper. Then we made our false retreat toward the woods, and they followed, believing we had had enough. When we had gone in far enough to have the undergrowth reaching for the legs of the horses we turned and had at them again. And the archers began again. Picking targets and silencing swords. I don't know how long it was, it seemed just a minute. I'm sure it was longer than that because I was near exhaustion when the last twelve men on horseback took off out of the trees and beat their horses wildly toward the castle.

And then it was done. We gave out a thunderous cheer and the archers poured down from the trees to join us. But the sense of victory lasted only a minute - the ground was covered with dead and wounded men. Blood and armor. Robin was shouting commands to get the carts and load the dead and wounded. "Quickly!" He kept yelling. Telling us we had to clear the field and abandon this place for the depths of the forest. Our force of thirty-five had suffered six dead, and five wounded. The enemy had thirty-eight men down of the fifty men that had accompanied the wagons. Of the thirty-eight, only twenty of them would survive their wounds.

Robin told us to take a quick survey of the downed enemy and see if we could help any of them. We spent ten minutes giving them what little help we could, then, with our carts loaded we set out. The wounded who could walk were placed at the front of the column, those who couldn't walk, and those who had died were placed on carts, also at the front. The rest of us followed slowly, at the pace of the hobbling wounded, into the shadows of the woods with Scarlett and two men far to the rear to warn of any pursuit. But there would be none. We were fairly certain of that. It would take time to mount a force and even if they did, no one, not even the arrogant Sheriff, would make the mistake of following us deep into the woods where one of us was worth five of them. It would have been insane. I was glad we were leaving the edge. It wasn't home and it wasn't safe.

Because keeping the secret of our base was the most important thing, we marched in the opposite direction of the camp, slowly, but steadily. Little John walked next to me, he had a deep cut on his left arm, it had bled heavily, which was actually good because it would clean well. Robin escaped serious injury, only a small cut on the forehead and one on his right shoulder. When darkness fell we made camp, feeling safe enough to build fires, which we huddled close to in our blankets. Robin came to me and asked how I was. I told him I was fine. "Surprise made the day." He said. He went to John. I heard him say, "You look tired." John said he was, Robin asked how was his arm. John told him it was nothing to worry about. Robin said to him what he'd said to me about the surprise. How much it had been to our advantage. John agreed that "Surprise made the day." Robin said "I'd rather another way, but all considered we did well." He waited for an answer. I saw there would be none. John was asleep. I followed his lead, glad to be alive.

****

When we came out of the forest into the great clearing we made a good bit of noise; feet tramping, carts and stretchers dragging on the ground, over the leaves and twigs. Alan-a-dale led us out. He was, like all of us, tired and moving slowly. Robin and Little John were behind him, then myself and the others, all pulling stretchers or carts behind us. Calvin and the archers came last – our clothes were bloodstained and torn, and we were damp again and the odor of us mixed with the air and I thought we must have made less than an impressive sight. I saw Cally look up from a tub of wash. She looked at each of us as we passed, she seemed to want to ask something but wasn't sure if she should. I thought to myself that we didn't paint much of a picture of success, more like a motley crew of a sailing ship that has just about escaped a sinking. I'd thought about war before, but on that particular day, coming home as we were, tattered and worn out, I was sure that the truth about war was that it's not very pretty, before, during or after. At best all it does is bring out a will to accept responsibility when the time comes to stand together. I saw no other redeeming virtue in it. Certainly gold wasn't a redeeming virtue. And I also knew then, and for sure, that it made changes in you that are permanent. Since that day every man I have known who has been in a battle has never been the same man he was before. I wish I could say that he was always a better man after it, but I can't say that, not based on what I've seen. Cally stopped Little John, he nodded and then kept on walking. I saw her head bobbing and weaving and as I passed her she whispered, "Patrick?" He was a favorite of hers, a happy man with a sharp wit and kind eyes. I shook my head, to tell her no, he is not dead, then she saw his body on one of the stretchers, wounded but alive, and then the body of Malten, still and white, so dead. And the other dead, they all had faces like statues, and were stiff and white. Hauling them into the camp like that – a long line of carts and stretchers - made me realize just how many there were and how bad it had been. It seemed worse now than when we had first loaded them. It seemed they had multiplied during the march, grown whiter, further away. Death had been a great rain on us. Gregory, who was one of those who had stayed to guard the camp, came to Robin and stared at him. It was the same look as Cally. He wanted to ask something but didn't know how to ask it. Robin was pulling a stretcher with the body of Willie Wilson, the camp joker. He and Gregory had been companions. He pulled out of the line, laid the stretcher down in front of Gregory and walked into the trees on the other side of the camp. Marion followed him with her eyes, then approached me. "Pen?" she said. I knew what she was asking without her having to ask it. I nodded and she moved quickly after Robin. When the final man was into the clearing they began to separate into small groups, tending to the wounded and preparing to bury the bodies of the dead. There would be no waiting on that chore. Everything would be prepared before anyone slept. The graves would be dug, the dead would be wrapped and laid next to the open tombs so that at first light we could have our service, place the bodies and begin to fill the graves. As I helped clean the cuts of the wounded, Cally went to Little John. She asked him, "Very bad?"

John shook his head, "Killing is never good." She turned to me, "Worse than expected?"

"Everything went perfectly," I said, "but after the first volley it was in the open fields. All hand to hand. Then into the edge of the woods. All considered, we were very lucky. It could have been even worse." I asked John if we should post more sentinels than usual. He said we should. Cally pressed her questions.

"But it was bad, very bad." I wasn't sure what she wanted us to say. It was as if she couldn't believe what she saw, would not believe it until we told her that what she was seeing was true. I guess it was necessary to hear someone say it had been bad. Perhaps then she could accept what it was. Maybe she needed someone to say it outright, and by saying it, accept the responsibility for it.

"It was very bad. But it had to be done." John said. She shuddered, looked at each of us.

"It seems like suicide, calculated, planned, suicide."

"Was battle ever anything else?"

"Then why fight? Why go?"

"You know the answer to that as well as I do."

"I hate it."

"We all hate it. Only a fool or a moron would like it."

"For gold! This for gold!" She waved her hand behind her at the dead bodies, "Is this worth it?"

I saw that John was becoming impatient, maybe angry with her. "Would you rather see them in the stocks then - or hanging from a rope? Or maybe running from village to village, hiding, afraid someone will know?"

"That's not fair John." She said. There were tears in her eyes. I'd never seen Cally cry.

"Yes it is. It's more than fair."

"You know what I'm saying, but this....this is never the only answer."

"It's been a good enough answer for them for a long time. And maybe the only answer they they'll ever have." John's voice was hard. I believe he'd had enough.

"Maybe, maybe not. I don't know." Her voice was fading. You could just about hear the end of what she said.

"Well, while you're deciding, maybe you could help me." John's cut was deep and ugly and was bleeding again. She helped him remove his shirt. I moved off from them, from the fire, from the wounded. Cally wasn't far off the mark. Gold wasn't much of a thing. A shiny yellow metal that you couldn't eat, couldn't drink. Yet, to do either you had to have gold, or you had to live in the forest where food and water was free. And maybe that was what she was trying to say. Why gold in the forest? If we were going to stay here, live out our lives here, what was the reason for dying for gold? Good question, I thought. No answer, I thought.

****

The following morning Robin and I began to sort through the booty and log the inventory of what had been taken. It was an impressive haul, and when the total was tallied and the announcement made there was a general sense of satisfaction. Someone shouted "It'll be a long time before all that's gone!" I looked at Cally, she smiled back at me. It was the same question in her eyes that I had asked myself last night. I wrote and recorded the names and amounts that each received and Gregory made the figures for what we would dispense in the villages. I suppose that part of it was good and sensible and maybe even worth it. I'm sure if you asked the villagers that were given the fifth we put aside for them, they would say it was the best thing that happened to them that year.

The first night after the burials was quiet. So too the second. The next was better, small groups of men formed around the fire and there was some laugher. Not the kind that we were used to, that would take time to regain, but there was a conscious attempt to return to something normal. Robin seemed pleased that our efforts had yielded so much, but there was no doubt in my mind that he took full responsibility for those who were gone – which he shouldn't have because it had been a vote and no one blamed him. The following night he and I sat at the great table with John, who said several times that it was a particularly good night, dry. John was not shy about talking, but he was also not necessarily someone who begin a conversation, especially one about the weather. I thought he might be looking for a way to say something about the battle, or at least to have us say something about it that might confirm how we truly felt. I followed his lead and agreed, it was a good night, there was a decided dryness, something that wasn't so common in the woods and always welcomed. John began to rub his arm and Robin asked about it. He said it was hurting more than he thought it should. I noticed a little trickle of blood running down to his wrist. Robin said that he might be getting too worn for this kind of life. John laughed and said it came with everything else a great fight brought, and we began to talk about the battle, and I said it might be best if it were a one time thing, and how it might be better to remain what we have always been - stay in the forest and make do with smaller encounters. "But it was a big prize." Robin said. I agreed it was, but now that I'd been in what I might call a real battle, I was one who certainly preferred the occasional purse, or smaller chest. Robin said he was sure all the men felt the same way, but they had performed brilliantly. "None of them are soldiers by trade. They're farmer's, merchant's, blacksmith's. But when asked to be soldiers, they rose to it." John gave no response, nor did I. There was none to give. It made for an awkward pause. Then Robin commented on the blackness of the forest and the peace of it. The long cool days, wet, but cool. The dark nights, and how the damp was bad for the bones. The good feeling of being close to a fire, the bad feeling of being drenched by rain dripping between the leaves and making the chill even worse. It was his way of changing the subject. I said, "Living in the city is dirty and crowded and sometimes evil but at least you have walls around you and a roof over your head." John disagreed and said that he thought the trees made good roofs and as for walls, he doesn't like the feeling of being confined. Robin said that he was too big for his own good and if he were a smaller man he wouldn't feel confined in a house with walls. John laughed and said that if he were a smaller man he would not be Little John. And then the conversation slacked. It seemed there was a reason for it to do so but I didn't know what it was. Robin rose to leave. John said he was going to leave in the morning to see Martha. Without turning Robin nodded, "Go see Martha. She deserves the time."

****

I don't know if it was a result of the great battle and the losses we suffered, or if it was that he felt responsible even though it had been voted on, or maybe it was just something he wanted to talk about and he felt the time was right. Whatever, it was the only time he ever brought it up. I'd have never done so. The fact that he was alone was his business. He never questioned who we were with or why, so there was no basis for us to treat him any differently. But once, and only once he broached the subject and never again. It took place a few days after John had left to see Martha. Men were healing and there was a quiet resolve in the camp. I was at the edge of the clearing listening to the birds. He came up behind me. This is, as best as I can recall it, what was said:

"Nice day."

"Yes," I said, "it is."

"I love these days, a little warmer, good, bright sun."

"Just about perfect."

"Just about." He pulled at a leaf, took it and tossed into the air, watching it slip and slide its way to the ground, did it again and I knew there was something on his mind. "Can I ask you a question, Pen?"

"Of course."

"You're still alone."

"I am."

"Why haven't you tried to find out about your friend, the one you said you were with?"

"I don't know. Just too lazy I guess."

"Lazy?"

"Well, maybe not lazy, maybe just don't want any kind of attachment right now."

"Easier being alone?"

"I don't call this alone!"

"You know what I mean!"

"If not easier, not harder that's for sure."

"I was always good at alone. Maybe that's why being here came easily to me."

"Maybe. But being alone can get tiresome."

"So you see the time when you'll want something more, someone."

"I do."

"I feel that way, sometimes."

"Then why not do something about it?"

"Not sure if I could?"

"I don't understand?"

"I don't know, just that I've always been comfortable enough alone, but maybe that's......." He picked another leaf and tossed it. I waited for him so continue, he didn't, so I said,

"Are you saying there's something wrong with that?"

"No, not that I know of, but......."

He seemed to be skirting what was really on his mind. I gave him plenty of time, but he didn't say anything, so I asked what it was that seemed to be on his mind.

"Nothing. Just rambling. Maybe still having a little trouble justifying what we did."

It was obvious he'd changed the subject for reasons of his own. "You mean the battle?"

"Yes."

"It was a vote."

"I know. My father said military men can't have a conscience if they're going to be good at what they do."

"That makes sense."

Marion was at the great fire, she turned and happened to see us. She waved and held up a tankard of ale, both of us shook our heads. She turned back to the fire.

"She's very pretty."

"Yes she is." I said. "If I were interested in women she'd be a candidate."

"No doubt."

It ended there. I have never had an answer. Marion would have been the best to give that answer. I never asked her.

****

The battle dimmed in memory.

In memory the battle dimmed.

Life lived in the clammy dankness of unending chill and shadowed light, returned to a deadening repetitiveness, a solidity that fell into a cadence that was like the movement of the slow growing oaks. The sense of loss that hung in the still air wasn't always there, and not always gone, but when it was there, it was a not so good memory, and when it wasn't there it seemed to be hanging just on the outside of the clearing, waiting to sneak back and make me remember. I hoped that it would never go away completely because then we would all have something to give us pause if we ever had the demon greed nudging at us again.

It was late morning when we heard the dry leaves crackle under the heavy foot of an approaching body. Little John strolled into camp. It was ten days since he left. A longer absence than any he'd taken since joining. Marion looked up from her sewing, and called out to him. He picked her up, and put a kiss on her cheek. She told him that he'd lost the smell of the forest. He nodded, "But that'll change soon enough. Tomorrow I'll be like everyone else." She put her arm through his and took him to the long oak table where she sat him down next to me. I asked if he'd been walking all morning? He had, and he said he'd done without eating anything since breakfast except a little bread and ale. Marion rose and said she would get him something. While we waited he kept scouring the campsite. I knew who he was looking for and he would find no sign of him. "He's not here." I told him. He asked where he was. I told him he'd gone to Shockwell with Gregory yesterday morning. He asked if the purpose of the visit was to check on Tuck. No, I told him, Tuck had passed through two days ago. He was surprised, saying that he didn't think Tuck would be on his feet for another week. It was supposed to be like that, I said, "but he had good reasons for taking to his heels."

"And what was that?"

Marion placed a large bowl of fruit, meat, an urn of ale and a loaf of bread on the table and I explained about a problem in the village with a woman. John wasn't surprised the problem involved a woman and asked what he'd done this time. It was the wife of the inn keeper where he was recuperating. John mumbled something I couldn't understand and then asked where he was now. I told him he'd gone to the monastery at Burnell, limping on a cane. "All the way to Burnell alone, with a broken ankle, on a cane?" I told him that Patrick and Alan-a-Dale had gone with him.

"When will Robin and Gregory be back?" I told him we expected them back tonight, if all went well. He continued to eat in silence, when he finished he asked me how I'd been and I asked about Martha. He said she was fine. Marion leaned over his shoulder, and told him he should marry that girl some day. He laughed and said that he planned to do so and she asked if the plan was to do it before he was an old man. She felt for Little John, as did I, because we both knew how much he cared for Martha, and how much he cared for Robin, and it was a wonder if he would ever live a life of his own so long as Robin roamed Sherwood. But it wasn't something you could say directly to him. You could hint at it and you could make vague suggestions, but he wasn't the kind of man and it wasn't the kind of subject you broach straight on. "You know Robin wouldn't mind." Marion said, just loud enough for it to be heard.

****

As Spring wore into the first early, warm summer days, we settled into the weather with pleasure, and watched as the lazy yellow light of a stronger sun turned brown into green. There had been no change in our numbers since the battle. It was the second day of June when Harold approached Robin with his request. They spoke for nearly an hour, then Robin left Harold at the great table and motioned to me to follow him. We stood at the edge of the clearing. He said that he'd begun to wonder if we would ever add to our numbers again. It seemed that we had become even closer, more isolated and more guarded since the great battle. I agreed that I felt the same way, as if we had, without planning it, closed the doors. He asked if that had truly happened or was it that we were just being very careful, maybe over reacting. "I'm not sure that any doors are closed, but yes, we've become a little more cautious." He asked why. I had no absolute answer. The battle outside had certainly sent signals. "What kind of signals?" "That we were safest and probably at our best inside rather than outside." The unasked question was whether that made the basis for a closed society. I didn't ask the question, nor did he, instead he said it certainly is apparent how great an ally the forest is. I agreed. "Pen, we have our place, a safe place, where we live as we choose. And if we should decide to make it a closed place, that doesn't seem much different than what we fled." There was truth in that, and it had the sting of hypocrisy, but we were no longer just a few people eating venison and building a fire in the middle of a forest. We had become known. And we had struck out against a Prince. And it did not matter that it was not because of politics, that we had not done it out of any desire to make a statement of defiance. It only mattered that it had been done. And because of it, we had to accept a new sense of danger. He asked if it were my decision would I say yes to this new man. I said that I thought it should be done by a vote. He didn't say yes or no to that and we made our way back to the fire. He took Harold aside and they talked again for some time. When it was over Harold was long faced, and Robin went off into the woods.

Little John, Tuck and Scarlett sat in a small group with Archie, Passy and Guthrie, while Alan-a-Dale played his flute. Several others lay on blankets, looking into the trees, watching the light play with the leaves. Others were passing the day in card games, conversations, and several had slunk off into the forest for intimacy. Reginald and Patrick spoke about going to the brook, a half hours walk, to wash. But regardless of what they were doing, everyone knew what Harold had asked and everyone wondered what Robin would do. Would he call for a vote, make it a communal thing, let the majority decide? Would he make the decision on his own, because after all, it was his forest. There was no conversation about it, no one voiced an opinion. No one would unless Robin asked for one. There was no question in my mind that saying no to Henry would be an unwritten declaration and there was something almost hypocritical about that, but at the same time something in my head said that saying no was the safe thing to do. When he came back into camp he spoke quietly to Little

John then circled the clearing several times while Harold sat unhappily alone at the far end of the table. When he finally stopped and approached Harold I knew it wasn't going to be a vote. He'd made the decision on his own and we would all live by what he'd decided. Alan stopped his playing and the other conversations came to a halt. It was several minutes before Harold bounded off and John, who had come to stand beside me said coolly, "He'll be in Shockwell and back before dark." As we watched him race into the forest I had the sense from his voice that he'd spoken against letting the man join. I asked him what he thought of it all. "Doesn't matter what I think. It's Robin's decision." I said that I had voiced my opposition. He smiled and said he was sure about that without having to be told. "I know you're careful, Pen. Always have been. You think more than most. People who think a lot are usually careful." I pressed him, "Then you approved of the decision?" He seemed hesitant about answering, so I started to walk away, maybe I'd pushed him too far. He called me back. "My head's against it." I was glad I wasn't alone, at least there were two of us, and I was especially pleased John agreed with me. He wasn't here because he needed a refuge and to me that made his thoughts important. "I'm here but I could just as easily be somewhere else. That's not the case for you, almost all the others. Up till now we've angered some people, pleased some others. But either way, we just weren't very important. No one went to bed thinking about the rejects in Sherwood Forest. Now that's changed. It's become dangerous, much more so than just a while ago. And we need to be more careful. I know you understand what I'm saying Pen, and you agree with me." He didn't wait for a response.

I had a conversation the next day with Robin. He initiated it and it was really more a monologue.

"I wonder if Tuck will ever settle down?"

"I don't know, he has a wanderlust. Have you ever seen him remain in one place for more than a week?"

"No."

"And John? When will he decide to marry Martha?"

"I don't know. He says he will, but he's very committed.......to....."

"To Sherwood?"

"Yes. And the men. And you."

"He's the right arm of us all, but we'd survive without him, if we had too."

"I know."

"Does he know that?"

"You mean does he feel free to leave if he chose to?"

"Yes."

"I don't know the answer to that."

"Neither do I. I wish I did. I'd like him to know his life is his to live. He owes us nothing."

"Why not tell him?"

"It would be an insult to do that.......have you noticed how well Gregory works the numbers?"

"Yes."

"Like a schoolboy."

"Yes."

"He could make a fine living in Nottingham."

"Yes."

"Kyle would make a good merchant. He has the gift of conversation and a sense of business."

"Yes." I saw the progression and feared the list of names was going to grow. I saw what he was thinking and the clarity of what I saw on his face made me all the more confused about why he'd said yes to Harold.

"This isn't so bad a life for some of us, but there's other things beside the forest."

"I know."

"You know more than you know. You know more than you let on. You do that a lot, Pen."

"Do I?"

"Yes."

"Is that bad?"

"No. But it does make me have to work hard at times to draw out your opinion."

"Are you doing that now?"

"I thought I was going to have to, but no, I believe I have it."

"I believe you do."

It was the first time I ever felt compassion for Robin, he wasn't the kind of man you felt needed compassion. But at that moment I felt it because it was the first time I'd ever seen him question himself and what he'd created.

Harold did return with Sean. A month or so after he joined us he became ill. It lasted several days and then it was gone. It happened again about a fortnight later. And then Harold took to an illness not unlike that which afflicted Sean. It wasn't the first time anyone had been ill in Sherwood, but something bothered me about it. It was nothing I could put a finger on, just a vague uneasiness in the way they had begun to look. Harold talked about going to Edmonton, to see an apothecary, but nothing came of it.

****

That year two incidents took place, both of which need to be told. That of Duncan and Cameron and that of Goneril.

We learned about Duncan and Cameron from Alan-a-dale when he came back from Shockwell. There was word about a burning that was going to take place in Nottingham. Two witches had been caught and confessed to crimes of perversion, casting of spells and theft. When the names were said Robin who had been feathering arrows jumped to his feet. I need not tell you why. I felt the same jolt, though obviously not so strongly as he did. He motioned to me and we walked some distance away from the center of camp. He asked if I thought it could be the same two. It was less of a question and more of him telling me he needed to know the answer and did I have any ideas. I told him that both were not uncommon names and the two men he'd told me about were certainly not witches. He laughed, "do you think half the burned are really witches, or more likely someone's enemy conveniently gotten rid of?" I agreed with him but that didn't bring us any closer to knowing if it was the Duncan and Cameron of his past. He paced and I knew without him saying it that he would not rest without knowing. He asked me if I would go to Shockwell and find out as much as I could. "According to Alan the burning is still a fortnight away. You could be in Shockwell by dusk."

I left within an hour and returned in the night two days later. What I'd found was that the two men were indeed the same two that he knew. "How can you be sure, Pen?" The complaint was witnessed by several prominent people among whom was "your step-mother Goneril."

"There's the real witch. She never stops! She's getting her revenge. Years later, but she never gives up! I've got to save them Pen, then I have to kill her!" I'd never seen him look like that. He reminded me of Tuck in his wildest moments.

They were being held in the Sheriff's lock-up and it was heavily guarded. We had a great asset in Will who had been a prisoner some time ago and knew the grounds and layout. No one asked Robin how he knew the men, nor why he had to rescue them. Everyone was willing to help, but he wanted only Tuck, John and Will. He said to me, "Pen don't be angry with me for keeping you out. You're a brave man, you've proven that many times over, but this needs men with less conscience than you. Do you understand?" I did and in fact I was glad he hadn't asked me to go because he was right, I might have hesitated when I should have acted and given where they were going and what they had to do, I'd have been a liability. I found out afterward from Tuck and Will what had happened.

The lockup was at the north end of the city, surrounded by a moat. The rear faced an open field and they made their advance from that field. They took a small raft to the foot of the lockup, and Will was hoisted onto the shoulders of Little John. He cleared the wall and then tossed them a rope. They came up and over and made their way around the tower to the gate. It was closed and there was a guard on the inside. Will had his short bow and killed the guard. Robin scrambled up the wooden gate, the top left ample room to squeeze between the gate and the stone of the tower. He came down on the other side and slowly lowered the gate just enough for the others to climb over. Inside the central courtyard they saw the tower and the small guard house off to the right. They made their way to the tower. Through the portal they could see two guards. Both were sleeping in their chairs. Will called out quietly so as not to be heard by anyone in the guard house. It was several tries before one of them woke. "Who are you and who the hell let you in at this time of night?" Will said he was bringing a prisoner and had encountered highwaymen on the way. When the man opened the door John dispatched him. The other came slowly awake and Tuck was on him before he could rise. Robin and Will walked the winding stairs checking cells while Tuck and John stood sentry. When they found the cell of Duncan and Cameron, they were asleep. Robin was the first one in, he woke each with a hand over their mouths. Once back into the yard Robin and Tuck remained on the ground while the others began climbing over the gate. It was then that a guard from the guard house mounted the terrace above the yard and saw them. He sounded the alarm. Tuck rushed the oncoming guards. There were five. Before Robin could reach him Tuck had killed two of them. Will said his sword whipped the moonlight around like a bird wildly drunk. Robin killed another and the other two fled. Tuck raced after them. Robin shouted to him to let them go. Tuck shouted back, "Can't. No witnesses to tie this to Sherwood." He caught up to them as they were opening the door to the tower, then he was back at the gate. It had all gone with incredible ease. They lowered themselves into the boat, took the short distance over the moat quickly and were on foot across the open field. When they reached the cover of a small grove of trees they stopped to rest. Robin and Duncan went off some distance and spoke for several minutes. Robin gave Duncan a purse with gold and sent them off.

During the following week Robin was in and out of the camp constantly. Restless, not talking much and obviously uneasy. Then it exploded, so to speak, and was in him like a demon and he couldn't rest until he'd dealt with it. Duncan and Cameron had done something to him. He was fueled by a fierce desire for vengeance.

A fortnight later five of us we were on the Cadbury road to that place Robin had once called home. I had asked to go with him. He was against it at first, but my incessant urging finally got him to agree.

Robin, was in the lead, walking alone. Archie and Alan-a-dale behind him and John and I behind them. He was making a torrid pace. I asked John what we should do.

"Do? What's there to do? He's probably years late in doing what he should have done."

"You think he should've killed her?"

"I don't know her, but what I know of what she's done makes her deserving of it."

"There's laws to take care of what she's done."

"Really? Well there's laws about a lot of things. Some of those concern me and you and the rest of the people in Sherwood. You don't seem to be in agreement with them."

"Unfair, John."

"You know what I mean."

"I do. But the truth is the truth."

"What's the truth?"

"Two wrongs don't make a right."

"There's also an eye for an eye."

"I don't want to argue with you John."

"Nor I with you. But it doesn't matter what we think. There's no stopping him."

"Maybe we aren't trying hard enough."

He looked at me and laughed. "Pen, don't say stupid things. You're smarter than that. And you know nobody's stopping him. If that's why you've come along, then do yourself a favor, turn around and go back to Sherwood."

We reached the edge of what was once his father's lands and now belonged to Goneril and her son. I tried to reason with Robin one last time. He wasn't listening. I asked him why. He said she was a murderer. I said she was, but killing her would make him the same thing. He turned on me. "Did you kill anyone in the great battle, Pen?" I didn't answer. "You did, we all did. We robbed and we killed. Now all of a sudden you have new rules? Not good enough. She's still hacking away. She'd do it to me if she could get to me. So I'm going to get to her first."

"Because of Duncan?"

"Because of what she's done. And because I owe it to my father." I wanted to challenge him on that. I wanted to ask him why he'd waited so long or why it had taken Duncan and Cameron to remind him of it. He looked at me, I was sure he knew what was in my mind. "I should have dealt with her when it was all happening. I didn't. I was younger then and maybe weak. I hid in the woods. I'm out now."

"And if you can do it. If it happens......."

"It'll happen!"

"If it happens, then what?"

"Nothing, I go home."

"And where's that?"

"What the hell are you talking about?"

"Where's home Robin? After this, where's home?"

"The same place it was before this, Sherwood Forest."

"I hope you're right." I turned from him and began the walk.

"Where are you going?"

"Home."

They came into the camp several days later. I tried to ask John without using words. He said nothing with his eyes, nothing with his lips. It was weeks later when I learned from Archie, who heard it while in Shockwell buying ale, that the wife of the late Earl and her son had to flee their home after a fire had ravaged the house. It was said the fire was started by robbers. I confronted John.

"When it came down to it he wasn't a murderer. We took them to the barn and held them while he set the place ablaze."

"What was she like?"

"Hard. Fearless. Didn't seem to care if she lived or died. Admitted she had Duncan and Cameron hunted down. She never forgot they had turned on her. She's a bitch. The son's a woman. Begged and cried for his life. He wasn't worth the killing."

"So now she'll be after him?"

"I doubt it. I think, in the end, she'd rather have Robin for a son than the one she has. It's over."

John was wrong about Goneril. Why and how you will learn. And maybe he was also wrong about what a murderer is. I'd come a long way since that first day in the forest. I wondered if I'd come the right way or the wrong way, or if there were such absolute things as right and wrong - or maybe it was just that people have a tendency to declare the absolute right and the absolute wrong to be what will best justify their actions. I wondered if God were watching, and how he felt about me.

****

During the two months that followed is when I began to notice it. It started with Sean, who, to my eye, was constantly pale. Several other of the men had come to complain of fatigue and a listlessness that would last a day or two. But it was Sean who was the one who concerned me the most. He'd developed a listlessness that bordered on constant fatigue and he'd lost a good deal of weight, and Harold, in the time since Sean had arrived, wasn't looking like himself. At first I blamed it on concern for Sean, but then it seemed more like a floating illness that overtook him a day or so at a time, then passed, then returned, at its own will.

On one particular morning, as the men sat at the great table there was a general joking pandemonium mostly contributed to by Guthrie who delighted in comedy. Morning in Sherwood, unlike dusk, was a come when you will process, and Albert, with the help of Cally, Marion, and Henry, made the food as needed until he decided it was done, then he removed the pots and late arrivers ate cold biscuits, bacon whose fat has congealed, and hard dry meat which is occasionally under the hunt of insects. Later that day there was the beginning of an illness that spread over the camp. Men had loose bowels and sour stomachs. Some complained that Albert had fed them bad meat. It was the first time I'd seen something sweep across just about everyone. Some were ill for just that day, but a good number were very slow to recover and some were sick for nearly a week. I'd not seen anything like it before and even John, who was normally even keeled and not prone to worry said that he'd not seen the like.

We all blamed it on the meat.

****

It was because of the man called Bertram that we finally and irrevocably became a closed society. He'd come to us bloodied, brought in by Archie and Calvin who had found him hiding in a bush at the side of Tear Drop Falls. Marion and Cally tended to him. He told us a story about thieves stealing from him and beating him on the Cadbury Road. Something about it seemed wrong, to me, something about him seemed wrong. We fed him and the following morning he was still asleep when I approached Robin at the great table and asked what he was going to do with him?"

"Do with him?"

"Yes. He's here. He knows the location of the camp. We have a rule about that."

"We do. And I know the rule. I made it. We've had that rule since the beginning and it hasn't stopped us from adding. Why is this any different than any other time? Why wouldn't he be welcome to stay with us if he chooses."

"And if he doesn't."

There was no answer. I reminded him that aside from those at the very beginning, Gregory and Henry, myself and him, everyone except for Marion, had been known to someone in camp before they were brought in, and it seemed to have served us well. This man was a complete stranger to everyone and in my mind and in the minds of some of the others that was a concern. "We don't know him, not at all. We know nothing about him aside from what he tells us. And it's been a long time since someone like him has......." Robin interrupted me and questioned what I meant. I denied that it had anything to do with the fact that he was obviously interested in women, not men. In fact, I took offense to what I saw as the suggestion that I was speaking against him because of that. "Then what is it?" Robin asked and I told him it was two things. One was the same concern I had when Sean came, that we needed to be careful. He said he was being careful. He asked for the second. I told him I didn't trust Bertram. He wanted to know exactly why that was. I had no specifics to give, just that something in my gut said he wasn't an honest man. He said I should not be so concerned until we knew if he was going to stay. "If he isn't going to join us, he'll be gone and you won't have to worry about trusting him." I was surprised at his response. If he were to leave we would be trusting a relative stranger with the secret of our location. I told him so. His answer was he thought Tuck would be able to make him understand the importance of being true to the people who had come to his aid. I wondered that threats might not weigh too heavily on his mind once he was clear of the forest. "What would you have me do? Make him stay, or kill him if wants to leave?" Robin had a way of always going to the core of it, sparing no words and leaving you exposed. Of course I wasn't suggesting that, he'd done nothing to warrant killing him. "I'm not saying that! I'm just uneasy, as I think you should be." Robin left me before I'd finished speaking. He'd never done that before. It seemed suddenly possible that there was more to it than just Bertram. I wondered if he regarded this man as some sort of a test. A focal point of what he thought might be a growing resolve to close off the forest to anyone else – to make Sean the last. To keep us what we were in size and spirit. Later that day he approached me and asked if I was speaking for myself or if I had the voice of others. I told him that I was speaking for myself, but there were a number who agreed with me regarding Bertram. "Regarding him, or regarding anyone else who might come along?" I said the discussion had never gone beyond just Bertram. I didn't get the feeling he believed me. Then he asked what we should do with him if he "says thank you for your help, I'm leaving now?" I had no answer to that other than we would have to let him leave. But, I added, letting him go knowing so little about him, worried me. "Maybe we shouldn't have brought him here in the first place." Robin fired back that the man was hurt and needed help and since when have we become indifferent to helping. I said, "We could have done that without bringing him here. Without exposing ourselves to him until we knew more about him." Again he turned on his heel, it was obvious he wanted the discussion ended. A few feet away he turned and said,

"If he asks to join us I'd say the problem doesn't exist. If he's planning on leaving we'll have a talk with everyone before any decision is made. Good?"

"Good."

He was eager to join us. At first his behavior gave no concern, but as time went on he became known to us as someone who drank too much and when he did he was loud and foul mouthed. At first we tried to ignore it, but it became too much for some of us, especially Tuck. On one particular night after he was asked by several to refrain and didn't, Tuck grabbed him by the collar and dragged him away from the fire. I couldn't hear what he said, but when Bertram came back he was pale and close-mouthed.

About a month later the incident with Cally happened. None of us saw because it took place at Tear Drop Falls. It was a warm August day and the air was especially moist. I was laying against a tree when Cally burst into the clearing. She stopped, then ran to me, falling against me in tears. I asked her what was wrong, when she collected herself she told me that she'd been in the water a short distance from the falls. She wore no clothes from the waist up. "The water was cool and if felt so good, Pen. Then I saw him approach. I thought I was alone. I sank myself down below my breasts and asked him to please move away. He laughed and said something lewd. I could see from his eyes he'd been drinking." She told me how he refused to move off and how he then made his way into the water, took her by the shoulders and tried to kiss her. She fought him off, ran to the bank of the brook, pulled on her shirt and raced back to camp. She asked me what she should do. I told her to say nothing to anyone, then I went to Robin. He listened, told me say nothing, we would wait for him to return to the camp. He did so before dusk. Robin approached him and they went into the forest some distance. Some time later Robin came out alone. He motioned to me to follow and we sat at the great table. He told me he'd admitted what he'd done and had been very apologetic, saying he had too much to drink and that being without a woman such a long time was wearing on him. Robin suggested he might spend some time in Shockwell. Bertram said that was a good idea and that he would leave in the morning for a few days. I jumped to my feet. We had our first real argument since I'd come.

"You trust that man in Shockwell! When he gets to drinking his mouth moves without the least concern for what he's saying?"

"He can be……."

"He can be dangerous!"

"We took him in by vote. We can't just say hey, you're a prisoner now because you drink too much and you can't control your mouth!"

"Yes we can, we have too!"

"Pen, do you know what you sound like?"

"Yes, I sound like someone who's sure this fool will make a mistake!"

"Ok, fine." He pulled his dagger and pushed it into my hand. "Kill him then, because that's the only way short of penning him up for the rest of his life, that you're going to feel comfortable about him."

I dropped the dagger on the table and started away, stopped and turned to Robin and said, "We made a mistake with this man. A big mistake. Now we're going to pay for it! I damn well wish Tuck were here!" Robin knew what I meant and as soon as I said it I regretted it. It was wrong to say it and wrong to wish it, the man had done nothing to warrant being killed. What he'd done to Cally was beyond excusing, but we couldn't kill him for it. In truth, there had been some episodes among the men that were not much different. But something was wrong and getting worse and as much as I was sure of it I saw no way to avoid it. And I wondered about Robin, who was always so careful. What was it about this man that made him lend out so much rope?

It was the only time I had argued with him, the only time I did not understand him. And I was angry. Looking back, because hindsight gives the almost perfect view, I still don't know why I was so angry. He hadn't said anything so wrong. In fact, he made perfect sense. We were in it as far as you could get and there wasn't much that could be done short of using the dagger. So why be angry at him? It made me think about Bertram and the fact that he wasn't like the majority of us. But then neither were the five. But I really didn't see them as being different from the rest of us because they'd been there for a long time and each of us had accepted the other. And maybe that was it. Maybe I had become a part of a new, exclusive club. The kind that sets membership rules. The kind that says who can join and who can't. The kind that has initiation rights and until you endure the initiation you're not accepted or trusted. But, if that were the case what was wrong with that? Don't clubs have that right? Can't a club that starts itself, takes care of itself, pays its own way, determine what the membership rules are? Hadn't we been doing that from the beginning? Hadn't it been agreed by everyone that secrecy was paramount, that everyone was everyone else's responsibility? That there were certain rules of conduct, and stepping outside those rules was not acceptable? It was all too complicated, it made me remember when my father had asked me questions that I couldn't answer because they seemed to have two opposite answers that worked equally well. Maybe Robin was doing the same thing. And worse yet, maybe the answer to every question is that there is no answer, just opinions. I gave it up, let it go before it got to haunting me. And I never again had an argument with Robin, not because I was afraid to, or because I'd be hesitant to disagree with him, but because I had gotten to a point where I wasn't sure of myself anymore. And until I could be, how could I argue what I wasn't sure of?

The next morning Bertram was gone before anyone woke. Not much was made of it. The camp knew about Cally and most thought he was ashamed of what he'd done and was happy to be off for a few days to let the memory of it fade away. It was near mid-day when Gregory came rushing out of the King's Building looking for Robin.

"He's with John out by the brambles, looking for grouse." I said.

"Pen, the gold is gone!"

"What gold?"

"Robin's future gold!"

"Are you sure?"

"Of course I'm sure!"

"Show me." He did. The box was empty. "I'll get Robin. Say nothing to anyone." Robin and John stood silent over the empty box, until Gregory said,

"Who?"

"Little doubt about that!" John said. I looked at Robin. He was hard faced, angry in a way I'd never seen him angry before. "He's easily out of Sherwood by now, maybe even to Shockwell!"

"Get your sword John, and let's go!" Robin and John left the camp, telling us to say nothing until they returned.

It was after dark that I heard them. They pushed through the edge of the clearing and into the light of the fire. Between them was Bertram, his hands tied behind him. Robin was carrying a sack that jingled and I knew it was the gold. Great murmurings began to fly around the camp, no one had known why Robin and John had left, now they quickly surmised the reason. Robin went into the building with the sack. When he came out he was still carrying it, but it was empty. He tossed it into the fire. He shouted for everyone to come close. When we were all around the fire he told them what had happened. The silence was frightening because it was alive and you could feel the anger in it. Robin waited several minutes before speaking again.

"It just remains to decide what to do."

"Kill the bastard!" Jonathan yelled.

"We have to vote!" Archie shouted.

"Vote hell, we all know what he tried with Cally, and he's a thief."

To me the money was the least of it. The man simply couldn't be trusted and we were outlaws, outcasts, and criminals by the laws of England. Our camp must remain secret and this wasn't the kind of man you could trust with that secret. Robin asked how many felt he should be hanged? Every hand but two went up. Robin moved so quickly you could barely see it happening. He and John were gone, into the woods, dragging the pleading Bertram between them. You could hear him begging until his voice faded into the dark. It wasn't long before they were back. Robin passed me quickly and stalked into the King's Building. John sat next to me.

"It's done?"

"Yes."

"Did he say anything?"

"Who?"

"Bertram!"

"He pleaded for his life. Said he meant no harm!"

"Meant no harm?"

"It was stupid, he was afraid."

"Is that all?"

"Robin asked him about his being in the forest, about the truth of his coming here."

"And?"

"He wasn't robbed on the Cadbury Road. He gave himself the bruises and the cuts. He heard about the ambush of the Prince's gold. Thought he might get his hands on some of it."

"Swine!"

"Now he's a dead swine!"

"It was a mistake to bring him here, and a bigger mistake to let him join."

"Bringing him here yes, letting him join, not really. If we'd have sent him off, he'd have sold us out. Letting him join just let him set his own trap for himself. His greed got him caught and in the end got him killed."

"I was never comfortable about him."

"I suspect you wouldn't have been comfortable about anybody."

"Maybe. You were right about what you said when Sean came in. Things have changed. We're not just a few perverted runaways making a little trouble any more. We've robbed the Prince's gold. We have to be very careful."

"Well you can rest assured of that."

"Meaning?"

"Nobody gets in anymore, nobody."

It seemed curious to me that it had come full circle. It also seemed necessary.

****

What happened with the boar was just another part of the proof of the treachery of life. How it turns on you when you least expect it, or are least capable of dealing with it. How it winds along its own path and cares little for your path. How it ignores the pleas, and demands payment for allowing you the breath you breath. How it tells you without telling you, that your only hope is faith in God and how he moves in strange ways.

We would hunt boar. It was as much for the challenge as for the meat. Venison is easy to acquire, Boar is much more a test of the hunters skill and the hunt was always done by a small group - the Boar can be ferocious when roused, lashing out when cornered. Its tusks are sharp and they use them like sabers. They are quick and their lunges are fearless. Robin had hunted boar as a young man with his father, and always the party brought with them the Alaunts, a powerful dog, to flush the boar from his cover. But in Sherwood we had no Alaunt, so our goal was to find the animal in the open.

Robin, John, Gregory, Reginald and myself rose early, with the sun still sleeping, the dew cold and glistening, the air still, wet with unseen water. We moved quietly out of camp. Reginald was an excellent tracker, and by mid-morning he'd found the trace. He examined the size and judged the animal to be fairly young but big enough to hunt. He was twenty yards ahead of us when he moved his left hand behind him, palm open, waving it toward the ground telling us to move slowly, he'd found the quarry. And he was correct about its size and that it was a younger male. He stopped and we moved toward him in an ever enlarging circle. The animal was eating in a small clearing with less than the normal undergrowth. He made a clean easy target for the bow and arrow, which is exactly the situation we wanted.

Robin, drew a bead and pulled back the bowstring. He was a second from letting the arrow fly when the boar raised its nose, jerked its head and suddenly lunged. Its keen sense of smell had found us. Robin let fly the arrow and it hit above the shoulder. There was a loud yelp of pain and the animal dropped to his side, but in an instant he was up, filled with rage, and lunging forward - directly toward Robin - who tried to maneuver out of his path. The animal whipped his head and we let our arrows loose - two missed and two hit the mark. But it didn't bring him down. The tusk slashed and hit Robin in the thigh several inches above his knee. He fell. The boar howled, blood pouring from the wounds, his head thrashing at the air. Reginald stormed out of the brush, sword over his head. The boar turned toward him, then it happened, very quickly before anyone could have done anything. He fell over a sapling that had fallen and he hadn't seen. He went down, tried to rise but could only get to his knees. We found later that his ankle had been broken. The boar lunged at him and drove a tusk into his stomach, he fell onto Robin, who shouted in pain as Reginald's weight dropped onto his leg. John had raced from the cover of the trees and with a single, wicked blow, nearly cut the boar in half. He hit the ground and was dead. Reginald's blood was falling over the cut on Robin's leg and then to the forest floor. I pulled at Reginald, then John put a hand on my shoulder, drew me back and picked him up. He laid him against a tree and turned to Robin. His face told the story.

Robin's wound was deep, a long and ugly one. John asked and Robin said, "I'm all right. See to Reg." John shook his head. There was no need to attend to him, he was dead. "Are you sure?" John nodded. I tore off my leather vest, then my woolen shirt and handed it to John.

"Wrap it with this. Try to stop the bleeding," John tied it tightly over the gash. It was nasty, jagged, like the kind that is made with a dulled knife.

"We need to get you back to camp." John bent to pick him up, but it was a long way back to camp and even for John it would be a struggle so I said that we should make a stretcher to take them both. While John stayed with Robin, Gregory and I went quickly to a sapling, hacked it down and began to strip off the branches. We did the same until we had enough to make a crude stretcher, enough to make the trip back to camp. We put Robin on one side, Reginald on the other. John moved the shirt from the wound, "The bleeding's slowed down." An hour later we entered the camp. Marion and Cally rushed to us. Cally asked how, and I said,

"Boar. Caught our scent and panicked. He caught Robin with a tusk before we could bring him down." She looked at Reginald.

"Is he dead?" I said he was. Robin had said nothing, the wound was still bleeding, but not as badly. The rag was removed and Albert, who had the most knowledge about herbs and medicines, looked at the gash. He told Marion to fetch water, and "put a pot on the fire. "It's deep. It's ugly. I'll wash it, and we'll cover it. Boar wound, infection's a risk." He looked at the body of Reginald, shook his head and told Marion to hurry with the water.

Infection is a dreaded word. An infected wound meant almost the certain loss of the limb, and if very bad, death. Most of the wounded men whom I'd seen die, died of infection as often as from the wound. Albert cleaned and dressed the leg, and applied a salve that he made from roots and herbs, the same salve I'd seen him use many times. The same salve I had seen have little effect if infection set in. And when it did seem to have an effect I was inclined to believe it was more the grace of God then the salve.

Robin lay on his back for the next two days and Albert attended to him with constant cleaning and dressing. It wasn't long before it began to take on a nasty appearance, and then began to ooze a white, gelatinous substance that Albert called puss! We knew what that meant. John and Tuck stared at the rings of blackened reddishness that had begun to ripple outward. And the smell. There was no denying the smell. As we talked Robin sweat like a pig, and twisted with pain. We moved away and Albert was the first to say it outright, but quietly so Robin would not hear.

"That leg has to come off."

Then the argument began about what to do and how. One of those arguments, the outcome of which, is decided before any words are spoken.

"No!" John shouted. I turned and saw Robin raise his head.

"Quiet! He'll hear us."

"He doesn't need to hear us, he has a nose."

"It has to come off." Gregory said.

"No, we can't do that." John repeated. "he'd never forgive us!"

"So we let him die and hope when he gets to heaven he forgives us for that?" Tuck said angrily.

"No, we don't do that either. We send someone to Shockwell for Parmon." I said.

Little John agreed, Tuck didn't. "You can't trust that man. You bring him here and we'll never be safe again. You saw what happened with Bertram."

We all knew the reputation, justified or not, of Parmon to be a great healer with great knowledge of herbs and roots. It was also said that he was a witch and brewed evil. Albert said he agreed with Tuck. Parmon wasn't a man to be trusted.

"We bring Parmon here blindfolded. He won't know how he got in or how to get back." I said.

"Why do we have to bring him here at all?" Gregory asked. "Can't you just go there and get something?"

"It's an infection. We need him here for as long as it takes to heal it."

"If he can heal it!"

"Why are you down on this, Tuck!"

"I told you, the man's a snake!"

Will Scarlett hadn't yet said anything. "Parmon's a dog, but it's either him, or the leg. And even with him here there's still a risk he won't be able to fix it. But we have to try something, and whatever we do, it has to be done soon. You can't waste time once it starts to smell."

"Robin said no one new ever again." John said.

"This isn't someone new being brought in. This is someone led in and out, blindfolded."

It had to be done. None of us could save the leg. Nor save Robin, if it came to that.

There was silence. John asked if we should call everyone together and take a vote. Tuck snapped that this wasn't the stuff of voting. It was a decision to be made by the man most worthy of making it. Then they all turned their eyes to me.

"You were the first to be with him. The decision should be made by you." Tuck said.

No, was all I said, then I said it again, no, I wouldn't make that decision alone. Tuck demanded that I make it. I said no again. I suggested John. John said no, let it be Tuck. Then Gregory said,

"There's seven of us here. Each say his choice and say it quickly. There's no time to waste acting like frightened women!"

Tuck said, "The leg."

John said, "Parmon."

Myself and the rest said "Parmon" Tuck didn't gainsay the majority. He said,

"I'll go right now."

"Scarlett and I'll go with you." I said. "If anything puts one of us behind the pace, the others keep up without regard for who's fallen behind. Agreed?"

Quickly we gathered quivers and bows and some dried meat and bread and then we were off.

****

I knew Parmon, or I should say I'd met him twice, long before I was discovered and forced to escape the village. I was sent to him by a man whose documents I regularly transcribed. A wealthy man, but a bit of a lunatic.

Parmon, was called a chemist, and sometimes a physician. In truth he was neither, rather he was a practitioner of the art of herbs and roots and certain other powders that were mysterious to most. He was the preparer of liquids and salves, from local growths, and from special plants and strange stuff brought from across the water. From France, Italy and the like. A strange and devious man, vehemently concerned with the acquisition of wealth beyond all other considerations. No one was sure about his true age, nor where he was born, but rumors persisted that he was nearly fifty, although his appearance suggested much younger. He was tall and lean, with long arms and very, very long fingers that are constantly moving, as if he was playing an invisible piano He was stoop shouldered and walked with a hesitating suspicious gate, his head stuck out like a bird looking for some unseen enemy. His voice, in contrast to his appearance, was softly melodic and spawned rumors that he could cast a spell of great strength just with that voice. Whenever he was asked about witchcraft he never gave an answer, he just smiled and let his fingers play the imaginary piano, while his body vibrated to the unheard notes. I always thought he was a liar and a cheat and that his actions were a performance designed to further the mystery of his reputation, but there were others, and many of them learned men, who thought he was some kind of special being with great powers of the mind.

He was also known to be highly sexed and was constantly attempting to coerce women, married or otherwise, and yet no one seemed willing to lay hands on him or to accuse him publicly. They feared his so called magic, his purported ability to cast a spell.

It's known for sure that he'd spent two years in Constantinople learning eastern medicine from dark and mysterious men with turbans and scars and close, beady eyes that never looked directly at you. But I do have to admit, in spite of how I felt about him, that much of what he brews in the steaming, gurgling black pots that sit like silent, aged black mushrooms above his constantly burning fires, have very often proven effective.

One of the greatest sources of his fame was that he was supposed to be in possession of an elixir capable of slowing the aging process, and supposedly many women give themselves to him in exchange for small vials of startlingly bright colors. But it remains a rumor because no woman has ever admitted to having given herself to him in an effort to get the liquid, and that makes it impossible to prove or disprove. On both of the occasions when I was sent to him I was brought into his laboratory. It was dark and gloomy, odorous and without any sense of joy or decency.

And It had sounds.

Bubbling sounds that never cease, even when he sleeps. There are rumors about that too, that when he is with a woman, he leaves the bed and opens a cabinet with a key that always hangs around his neck, and which he never parts with. He supposedly drinks something from a vial in the cabinet and then takes on a strange odor. When he climbs back into bed he is supposedly renewed with a force that provides pleasures unknown from any other man. Probably another rumor which he started himself.

I know from the man who sent me to Shockwell to buy from him, that he keeps a diary in which he records information that he believes might be salable to interested parties, most especially the nobility. His ability to read and write Latin and Arabic have added to his reputation as an important and learned man whose powers should not be taken lightly and have gained him a considerable amount of financial success and even a limited respect from many of the wealthy of Nottinghamshire. I have no use for him. This is what happened the night we went to take him back to Sherwood.

****

We stood rigid while Tuck slammed the door of Parmon's cottage

No answer.

He slammed again.

"Who?" The voice seemed to come from the back of the cottage.

"Tuck."

"Tuck?"

It wasn't a question, neither was it a statement of recognition or acceptance.

"Yes you fool, Tuck!"

"Wait a minute."

Tuck drummed his fingers along the wooden jamb of the door, then looked back toward Will and I, who stood in the shadows of the large tree whose branches arched out over the thatched roof of Parmon's cottage. I confess to having been uneasy. And although I'd never believed him to be a witch capable of spells, there was a certain aura in the air that made my stomach quiver. We heard the wooden bar being removed from behind the door, it swung open and Parmon stood before Tuck, half dressed, holding his pants up with his right hand, his left hand on the door, his eyes drawn together, his eyebrows twitching, and a sudden strange smell that began as soon as the door was opened. I saw the moonlight on his body which had the look of someone covered in oil. There was a chain around his neck with a key hanging from it.

"Tuck, it's the middle of the night."

"Not yet, not yet. It's ten."

"Still too late."

"I need help with a wound."

"Help with a wound?" I could see his eyes narrow. "Anyone I know?"

"Shut up, stop the questions and get ready to go with me."

"I have company!"

"Get what you need, put on some clothes. No time to waste."

"Impossible."

"Absolutely possible. You'll do it or you'll die!" Tuck drew his sword from his scabbard, it made a softly whirring sound. Of all those whom he knew feared the stories of his magic, Parmon knew Tuck didn't. He also knew that Tuck would not hesitate to run him through.

"I can't cure a man without my potions!"

"Take them with you!"

"There's hundreds. I can't take them all. Bring him here and I'll work on him."

"He's not coming here. You're coming with us. Get what you need and be quick about it!" He brought the sword to the belly of Parmon.

"I'd have to guess what to take."

"Then guess and guess right because if he dies, you die!"

"I'll need to know what kind of wound?"

"Why?"

"To treat it properly."

"You don't need to know that. A wound is a wound."

Parmon seemed to stand a bit straighter, his voice seemed to take on a surer tone. "I don't tell you how to wield that sword. Don't tell me how to wield my cures!"

"A gash from a boar delivered close up, like one you'll have, if you keep me here any longer."

"I'll get what I need." He turned from the door and shuffled across the dirt floor of his cottage, grumbling under his breath, the keys that never left the ring, that never left his person, jingled as he walked. Tuck turned to us.

"You heard?" I said we had. "He's a vile piece of shit! I hate being within ten feet of him!"

Then we heard it, "Parmon, what are you doing, who's at the door?" A woman's voice. Tuck pushed the door fully open and leaned his head into the cottage. We heard Parmon.

"I have to go, and it has to be now!"

"You promised me!"

"Shut up!" Parmon shouted.

I thought I saw a look of recognition on Tucks face, as if he knew the voice. Several more minutes passed, then Tuck pounded against the side of the cottage with the hilt of his sword. Parmon returned with a large pouch slung over his left shoulder. Another smaller one over his right and a leather bag in his left hand.

"Certain you have what you need?"

"Yes."

"You'd better be sure."

"Take me to him."

Tuck turned to us. "Let's go!"

Parmon peered at us through the darkness. "Who are you talking to?"

"My friends, who'll help me chop you up if you fail!"

****

I was certain then, and I'm certain still, that the night we pulled Parmon from his den he didn't know for sure that Tuck was a part of the band of outlaws who had already been accused of ten times more than they had done. I'm sure he'd heard rumors of the kind, but he had no first hand knowledge and as he was well aware from his own comings and goings, rumors are sometimes true, and sometimes false. But, I'm also sure that suspicions began to turn to almost certainties not long after we began our march to the forest. And when we stood at the edge of Sherwood and Tuck wrapped a hood around his head I believe he became positive that he was being taken to the outlaw camp. There are those who disagreed with me those many years ago, and probably there are those who still do, but I was there and I saw what I saw and heard what I heard and I stand by my assessment. Whatever the case, when we walked into the camp it was nearly day break, Albert was astir and the fire was crackling and when the hood was removed his bony fingers began plucking the unseen piano and I think he saw an opportunity of great proportions opening up before his greedy, beady, eyes.

He was led to Robin. We watched as he asked for a fire to be built and as he hung several small pots over it. He mixed and boiled again and again. He pulled small bottles from his sacks and added liquids and powders to the pots. He moved around them as one possessed, lightly, almost above the ground, his head turning down constantly to smell what was brewing. He said nothing to anyone and none of us spoke to him. Men came and went, keeping a distance, but overwhelmed with curiosity. Cally and Marion watched from a distance and once Marion came to me, tugged my shirt and said, "the devil moves inside that man." By mid-morning he appeared satisfied with the results of his work and he began applying the results from the pots in layers to the wound. There were two days of the same behavior and strange smells in the camp. Two days of the disconcerting face and form of Parmon. Two days waiting to see if he could effect a cure. Each night he was put into a lean-to and guarded. He drank huge amounts of ale and ate huge amounts of food. I wondered how a man could eat so much and remain so skinny.

On the evening of the second day Robin seemed no better, but he also seemed no worse. Tuck demanded to know.

"Well, it was a bad one. I'm doing my best, but it was a bad one."

"You've been mucking around for two days and that's all you can say!"

"It's all I can say because it's the truth. It's a bad one because you waited too long. You should've come to me sooner. You've made my job ten times harder. You've made his risks ten times greater!"

"Maybe we did. But that makes your life ten times more worthless than it's ever been!" Tuck poured a goblet of ale. Parmon sat quietly, occasionally glancing at Robin, who was asleep. At length he began to vibrate, the hands began to move. "Stop the twitching Parmon."

Parmon made an effort to sit motionless but I was watching him closely and I could see it was beyond him to remain still. His body simply didn't know how to come to rest. He turned to Tuck.

"It does get lonely here, doesn't it?"

"What?"

"For someone like you, it must be difficult."

"Why?"

"Company."

"Company?"

"For a man…you know…who wants a woman. I've heard that this is not the place for men who like women. Not the place for men like you and me."

"You and me! There aren't two living things more unlike than you and I!"

"Maybe, but we share one thing in common. We both prefer women."

Tuck turned on him and grabbed him by the throat. Parmon let out a great shout. I rushed to them.

"Tuck, we need him alive!"

"These are my friends! Killing you for insulting them would give me great pleasure! And killing you without a reason would still give me great pleasure."

"Tuck!" I reached for his arm. He looked angrily at me, then relented.

"I know. I know." He released his grip and Parmon coughed and wheezed. Tuck spit on the ground at Parmon's feet. "You're a foul man. Ending your life would be a blessing to the world." He stormed off.

"Can you cure him?" I asked Parmon.

"It's a bad one." His eyes searched for Tuck. Then he looked quickly back to me, "But he'll be fine in the morning." I wondered at the difference in his response to me, the sudden assurance. From what I saw, although not visibly worse, Robin was certainly no better.

When I woke the next morning there was a stirring in the camp. I jumped to my feet. A crowd was around the great table. I sensed it. I pushed my way in. Robin was sitting at the table eating. I glanced down at his leg. The ugly red-black rings were gone. Disgusting as he was, Parmon had done the impossible. I couldn't believe it. I looked for John, caught his eyes and he shrugged his shoulders. Tuck came up behind me. I turned to him. He smiled.

"Well, the evil bastard did it, no denying that!"

"No, no denying that. What now?"

"Put the hood back on and get him out of here. He's learned too much already."

Parmon protested that he was hungry and deserved breakfast. Tuck told him to shut up, shoved a piece of bread and some dried meat into his hands, told to eat quickly and when he'd done so, tied the hood in place. He was led out of the camp by Tuck and Scarlett. I heard Parmon complaining as they left, "What about something to drink. I need something to wash this down. What about some ale!"

During the next two days Robin recovered quickly. Parmon had left two salves which were to be applied until they were gone and a vile that he was to drink twice a day until empty.

Regardless what happened after those two days. No matter what Parmon did, what Thoren did, what the Sheriff did, there was no denying that the bony, vibrating skeleton of a man had worked a wonder before our eyes. A wonder I have never seen before or since. Never have I seen a man with an infection so severe, keep the limb and keep his life. Regardless what is said about him, regardless what I feel about him, and what I was a part of with Tuck, Parmon saved the life of Robin Hood during those two fateful days.

Thoren:

My name is Thoren. I was a knight in the service of the Sheriff of Nottingham. I served him as any knight would serve his lord – obediently, though he didn't deserve it. About me, you need not know much more. About him, the Sheriff, there is much I can, and will tell you. I knew him better than most.

I have been asked to write this because I was there and was privy to things no one else could know, and because I was caught in the politics of it, which didn't interest me at the time and after all these years, still are not my concern. A hundred stories have been made up about it, and about Robin Hood and his collection of perverts. Most of them are stupid, or just plain lies. The people who have the most to say are usually the people who were not there. Most talkers are that way, writers too, they know everything, but they know nothing. And even if they had been given the chance to be a part of what they write about, they would have said no thank you because being there takes courage and the talkers are the ones without the courage. I did this only because the man called Pen came to me, and because I make no denial that Robin Hood was a better tactician than most I have gone against. But I'm no writer, and I hate those who are because, as I said already, they write about things they have never done, make judgments about people who could kill them in seconds and are generally weak drinkers, loud mouthed and too full of themselves. Nonetheless here it is, what I know from being there, what I know about the last battle in the forest and the end of Robin Hood.

I was with the sheriff when he had his audiences with the Prince, and then with Parmon. The meeting with the Prince went badly for the Sheriff. I was glad for that. The Sheriff started out by saying that Robin Hood was just an irritant. The Prince screamed at him that he was far more than an irritant! The Sheriff apologized, said he should have chosen a different word. Regardless, there was going to be no calming the Prince. He screamed about the hundreds of pounds of lost gold and silver. He stormed the room. He told the Sheriff "if to you it's merely an irritation, then you can refill my coffers by emptying yours!" That wasn't an option so far as the Sheriff was concerned. Not even to keep his Prince happy. For me I could have cared less about the amity of this Prince, this so-called temporary king. This short, stocky, round-faced, dark eyed, compassionless man that showed little in the way of sympathy or compassion to anyone. A man who changed his mind and his loyalties to best suit his own gain. A man who drank too much, ate too much and spent too much time with women. An empty hearted buffoon to my way of thinking. Someone easy to despise. But the Sheriff always played the fool to him. He said it was better to do that than be foolish enough to force a match of power – a contest he had no chance of winning. As the Prince stalked the room like a madman, the Sheriff continued to apologize and excuse himself, excuse his words, the very fact that he was alive. "Anything, my Prince, anything I can do." Disgusting performance. The Prince said he was to immediately see to the recovery of the gold and silver and the destruction of this outlaw. "Right now!" He brought his ugly beak nose up to the Sheriff's face. "This instant, as we speak, not tomorrow, not the day after tomorrow, not next week or next month. Now!" I hate his high pitched whine of a voice. "Get it back, or I'll have it from you and then I'll send you to your grave." The sheriff said he would do as he was told. "Don't just yes me! Get it done. Capture him. Kill him! Kill his whole band! Die trying. But do it!!" He stormed out. I thought how much I would enjoy running him through.

Yes, the outlaw was a nuisance, the Prince was right about that. Maybe even more of a nuisance if you add in the gold and silver he takes. But the truth is he made no great trouble for anyone beyond the travelers he pilfered. Or the wagons he might waylay in the forest. The only time he caused a serious disruption was the taking of that tax money. I thought it was a stupid thing for him to do, he was having a fine time with the petty theft, why ruin it by angering a Prince, even if that Prince was a fool! Why cause a work up when everything was so easy for you?

The damned fool had gone and sealed his own fate by virtue of his own greed. Not a smart thing to do. I would have thought a successful thief knew better.

Of course when the Prince is gone he turns on me. "He's adamant about this outlaw. I have to have Robin Hood, or his head, I don't care which."

"How? He's deep in Sherwood, we have no idea where. They live it every day, know its moods, its colors. It stretches for days in every direction, it's a silent, dark, blanket of doom for anyone who goes in there after them. They proved they can fight by nearly wiping out the whole caravan escort. They have some of the best bowman in England sitting in trees and killing at will. And we have no idea where the camp is. What do I do? Take fifty men in, wander around like lost sheep while they pick us off one by one? We'd be easier targets than those at an archery contest. All these perverts do is steal from travelers, they do us little harm."

He screamed about what the Prince had just said. "He's not going to take no for an answer!"

"Maybe not, but you're not going to get his gold back by sending me in there to get slaughtered!"

"What's my choice?"

"Information."

"Information?"

"Yes. Information. We need to know where the camp is to have half a chance."

"How the hell do I find that out?"

"Let it out that there's money, a lot of money for anyone with information. Without information he's beyond reach in that black hole of a forest!"

"I'll do what I can. I'll do whatever money can do. But before the winter sets in you're going after him. Information or not!"

****

A fortnight later the Sheriff summoned me. He would be able to get the Prince off his back. He told me he had information. It involved Parmon.

Parmon, as I knew him, was a disgusting, dirty man, with a reputation, among other things, as a healer. It seemed foul and unjust then and still does now, that such a man as Parmon could be the undoing of men, who although they were outlaws, and perverts, had shown their courage in the open field. That cowards, cheats and blackmailers can hold the fate of men who are willing to die in battle was, and is, a disgrace. We talked. I was less assured than the Sheriff, less thrilled about what he'd found out. First, I suspected the possibility of false information deliberately given up to lure us to an ambush. For me, it was completely possible that Parmon was collecting at both ends. Second, even knowing where the camp was didn't change the fact that the closest point of entry to it was still two hours march inside the forest. Thousands of trees and thousands of places to ambush us.

"You'll move quickly, eliminate the chance he can ambush you. You'll be on him before he knows you're there."

"Stupid! How stupid are you? You don't think he has the place covered with sentinels? You think he just stumbles on travelers by accident? He knows what's going in those woods better than you know what's going on in your own manor house! You think he won't know about a column of men trampling through the woods before we get to him? Stupid!"

"Don't call me stupid! Just do what you're told! You wanted information, I got you information. Take as many men as you need. Overwhelm him with numbers."

"In other words sacrifice them."

"Let them die for their country!"

"You've said some stupid things in the years I've known you. But that's more than stupid."

"I told you not to talk to me like that!" I laughed at him. He was only a little less pompous than his pompous Prince. He'd threatened me a hundred times before and knew that threats and shouting was all I'd take from him. Anything more would be a mistake. He drew breath and paced. Then he cooled and put his hands on my shoulders the way he always did when he was trying to lure you into something for his own benefit. I hated that about him. "I need this. I need it badly. Let's talk about this logically." Logically meant how much is this going to cost me to get you to do what I want you to do. Idiot that he was he never in all the years figured out that I would have done it without a bribe. I lived by the sword. My food came from the sword, the women, and the money. And I'd long ago pledged I would die in battle long before I would let myself become what he'd become. For me war was life and life was war. And because he lived only for money, he could never understand that. Long before the price was as high as I knew he was willing to go, I said "Yes I'll go." The simple truth of it is, always will be, that true glory is in the willingness to go. Any man can die if forced by conscription, but for the man of the sword the glory is in the willingness to go. To go with the burning breath of the bull pouring from your nostrils, the air alive with the singing of swords and arrows, without that, there is little to live for. War has been the only romance in my life, the only thing that made my heart sing. Of course I'd go! That idiot had no idea what a man is.

I prepared my plans quickly. The winter was approaching, and I would not chance a march and an attack in the grip of cold, wet weather. Knowing the location of the camp provided the opportunity of choosing an entry into the forest as close as possible to the target, but that was just a foolish waste of men. I decided that the best chance would be to have two columns. One entering at the west, as close to the camp as possible with forty men, while the other, sixty men strong, entered from the north west, a mile above the larger force and half an hour later. My plan was that the first force, the smaller, would get the attention of the sentinels, Robin Hood would quickly surmise that we had learned the location of the camp and he would move quickly out against them. I was fairly certain the first column would suffer heavy losses and that afterwards the outlaws would begin a triumphant and relaxed march back to their camp. We would be waiting for them. It would all start in the early morning, just as the sun rose high enough to give sufficient light. No armor would be worn and no horses, all on foot, light garments only, not good protection from arrows, but very suitable for movement in the woods. The forest, in the underbrush and oaks, was no place for a knight's armor and a lumbering horse.

I kept the plan and the target a closely guarded secret, saying only that we were marching to provide escort for a royal shipment, and would be divided so that the larger force could guard the flank of the smaller. I gave up my trust to no one. It was important to be very, very careful.

Cornelius:

We were around the table when the first sentinel came rushing out of the woods. The second came less than a quarter of the hour later. What they said told us that a column of forty men was moving in a line which would bring them directly to the camp. All on foot, no armor. Not using trails, crumpling the undergrowth. There was no mistake they had a destination in mind and we were that destination. Somehow they seemed to know exactly where, in the darkness and the doom of it, we were. Tuck cursed "that bastard Parmon!" Saying we should have killed him while he was here. "The worm's signed our death warrant." John questioned how that could be, he was blindfolded in and out. Archie said he was a witch.

"No. No witch." Robin said calmly. "He took his bearings some other way. He had two days and two nights to do it." He's smarter than we were. But he's no witch." Tuck pulled out his sword, dropped it on the table, dragged the grinding stone close and began to work the blade. John asked if we had time to move out and be on them in the woods, before they reached the campsite. Robin didn't respond. John asked if he should call in the other look-outs? Robin still gave no answer. John looked at me, confused. He motioned to me to say something. I shook him off. Some time passed. None of us moved and Tuck kept the wheel going. The sound of the blade on it was ominous. There was an expectation and a nervous silence covering the camp like a blanket. Every minute seemed like a minute of lost surprise. When Robin spoke he was calm voiced. "I think there's more than that column." We looked at each other. I asked what he meant. He went on without answering my question. "If we call everyone in, then move against the column, there won't be any lookouts. If there's a second column they can move to the camp and be waiting for us." It was a chilling thought. He paced the table twice, then told Gregory to take two men and get out to Mermaid Creek. "You're looking for the second column. You need to find it if it's there, and I'll bet it is, then get back here within an hour. Can you do it?" Gregory assured him. "Good, get going!" He told John to get the map. John spread it on the table. Robin studied it. "Here's the first column. Look here, to the north, Mermaid creek. It follows down, then moves east. If a second column were to follow the creek, then, where it bends, move back to the south, they'll have a direct line to the campsite. I believe there's a second column and I believe that's what they're planning to do.

"You're sure?"

"No other reason to send forty men tramping into the middle of an ambush unless you want them ambushed." Tuck listened and kept sharpening. "We'll be in the trees, along both routes." He turned to Calvin. "Very high, higher than we ever have. You need just enough of an opening to get the arrows off." He turned back to the map and began making marks along both paths. "Put a man at each mark. We'll pick them off like rabbits. After they've passed, everyone stays in the trees until you signal them down, and you don't do that until I signal you. Understood?" Calvin gathered the maps and the archers and was gone. Less than an hour later Gregory was back telling us Robin was right. A second column.

"Sixty men. They've pulled up at the creek. It's Thoren in the lead, and he's pacing like a madman. I'm sure he knows something's wrong."

John seemed troubled. "Thoren's no fool. It would've been better if they had someone else leading."

"He's leading *because* he's no fool."

"You think he'll come straight to the camp?"

"Absolutely."

"This is all Prince John."

"Of course it is!" Tuck said. "The sheriff doesn't have the courage or the will. He must've been pushed into it. Too bad it's Thoren. He isn't a bad fellow. Too bad he has to die in the woods on the Prince's business instead of dying for Richard." He kept on with the sharpening of his sword, the sound of the heavy blade against the stone. "Parmon. Parmon. It all starts with Parmon."

"No matter now, this had to happen some day. We'll take care of business first. Later we'll worry about who needs to be dealt with. Keep sharpening Tuck!" Robin smiled. "But if everything goes right you won't need that blade today."

Thoren:

I have to admit it. I thought there was little chance the bait would not be taken. I was wrong. I misread the outlaw. He was shrewd, much better a military man than I'd imagined. He acted with calm and with a knowledge of tactics that I'd never have expected from someone who wasn't a professional soldier. I respected what he'd done. But that didn't change what I had to do. I was in the woods with one hundred men and I was far too committed to turn back. I was uncomfortable, but with no choices. Staying put was senseless. We either had to move out of the forest or move to the camp and attack. Moving out was just as dangerous as moving forward and didn't even offer the possibility of meeting the enemy face to face. All I could do was adjust my plans and move against him. I rested the men and formed both columns into one. We were in one of the most densely treed parts of the woods, dark and wet with a creek in front of us, and little room to maneuver, an easy target for archers. I decided to move to the campsite as quickly as possible. There was a chance he'd planned on us leaving when we realized he'd not taken the bait. I sent five men to the far front and five to the far rear and we left the creek behind us. I thought it was no more than half an hours march to the campsite. Now we were bait again, but without the benefit of a plan. Five minutes into the march the whistle of an arrow, a man fell. Then another and a second man was down. Then silence. I halted the column and waited. Nothing. There was no room to take any type of defensive posture and the trees stood so tall and dark that whatever formation we took we were completely vulnerable from above. I cursed the Sheriff and his Prince for sending us here and then myself for underestimating the outlaw. I'd not seen the forest for the trees. There would be no glory this day, and dying at the hands of a band of outcast deviants would be a disgrace. I ordered the column forward and several minutes later another man fell. It was a slow and deliberate slaughter and there was little I could do about it. We did reach the clearing in half and hour and it had cost us fifteen men dead or wounded, but once there, the arrows ceased. We tended to the wounded, the dead I'd left on the forest floor.

The site was deserted of course, not a person, not a piece of clothing, not a morsel of food, only a spent fire. We searched the lean-to's and the large wooden building. Empty. We hadn't planned on being in the forest overnight and had little in the way of provisions. I ordered a hunting party to find deer but cautioned them to stay close to the clearing. We built a large fire and sentinels were posted. An hour later two of the hunting party returned. They had several rabbits and some grouse, hardly enough to be a satisfactory meal after a day of marching. Three of the men sent to find food had been killed. It was a long night, but without incident. At first light I ordered a forced march out of the forest. It was obvious there would be no confrontation with the outlaws and remaining a minute longer was of no benefit to anyone. I knew what the march out of that hell hole would be. And only once did we see even the slightest trace of what appeared to be a man in the trees. We fired at him but it was useless.

They killed us from afar and there was nothing we could do. I tried to put order into the chaos that was building, and the arrows continued to reign down. There were shouts for help from the wounded, and groups of men rushing several feet in one direction, then as an arrow whistled into one of them they turned direction and ran toward another arrow coming from somewhere else. It happened again and again. They began to break, to scatter through the forest, thrashing through the undergrowth but there was no place to go. Then the arrow buried itself into my thigh. I couldn't help but smile at the skill of this general, this Robin Hood, who knew his land and its strengths and the strengths of his men as well as anyone I'd ever fought against. And there in that cold, damp place we were humiliated. I'd never been in such a battle where there was seemingly only one side to it. Never been vanquished so easily. Never felt such a fool. I'd expected troubles, losses, but nothing like this. We hadn't killed a single one of them. I swore then that I'd never go against these men again. Not out of fear. Those who later said it was, can believe anything they choose to believe.

By the time we reached open ground the count of lost and wounded was forty-two. I was disgraced and angry. More at myself than anyone else. My pride had made a decision that my ability couldn't live up to. The sheriff was insane with anger. "What do I tell the Prince? What do I tell him! A hundred men went into the forest, twenty-seven were killed and fifteen wounded - and that's all! That's the sum total of what was accomplished!" I gave no answers, there were none to give. I'd gone against a superior tactician and lost. My plan had failed. I'd had enough of this arrogant pig of a Sheriff. It had been too many years listening to his stupid shouting and ridiculous ideas. It was only a short step for me to make my decision. I left England for France not more than three months later.

I've put all this down because he asked me to do so. "So that it might be complete." He said. I understood from his first visit that Marion, the woman who was closest to Robin is also in France. I have never met with her. I have no desire to. I have not left France since arriving, and I never will. England is no longer my home.

Cornelius:

We had come into the clearing once the signal was given, which was nearly an hour after Thoren had moved out of the forest. It was a quiet entry, no celebrating - no shouting, no cheering. We were happy, of course, we had just defeated a great force without the loss of a single man. But there was the complete and definite realization that we were not immune from direct attack and certainly no longer ignored.

Robin was standing in front of what had been the fire the enemy had burned during the night. It was being re-stoked by several of the men. John and Tuck were some ten feet from him, talking quietly and I was with Marion and Cally. The sound was unmistakable, made even more so by the quiet in the camp. I looked up toward the trees past the fire because it seemed to come from that direction. It was done before anyone was truly aware of it. Robin bent over, then fell to one knee. John and Tuck seemed stunned, then raced toward him. The shaft of the arrow protruded from his side. A second sound broke the air and John pushed Robin to the ground and covered him with his body. The second arrow flew so close that it tore a line in the leather of John's vest. Had he not pushed Robin to the ground it would have hit its mark. Tuck shouted, "There, above the King's house!" I looked into the trees but saw nothing. I looked to Tuck, but he was gone, into the woods. John picked up Robin and carried him to a tree and sat him upright. He called for Albert to bring some water, then he pulled the arrow out. It didn't seem a fatal wound, but neither was it insignificant. We all gathered around Robin and John. John told Will to take five men and post sentinels and the others to arm and stand ready at the edges of the clearing. I said to John,

"Thoren's an hours march away."

"I know, but the arrows didn't shoot themselves. Somebody drew a bowstring."

Albert tended to the wound, then we took Robin inside the King's Building. John told him to rest, but he wanted information. We had none to give. "We'll take care of things. Just relax." He motioned to Albert to stay with him. Outside he asked Marion and Cally to see to whatever help they could be. It was the return of Tuck about an hour later that captured the attention of everyone.

He was alone. I asked if he'd found anyone.

"No." He asked to see the arrow. John handed it to him. He turned it over in his hands several times. I could see in his eyes that he knew something we didn't.

"Thoren left someone in the trees." Will Scarlett said. Tuck said Thoren had nothing to do with it. The man that fired the arrow had nothing to do with Thoren. He was there to wait until Robin was in the open. He seemed very sure of himself. We were all open mouthed. Tuck said, "I know how he works. Just for the money, cause is nothing to him." John asked what made him so sure. Tuck tossed the arrow back to John. "This is Potelle. The Sheriff's one to take full advantage of a situation. And he took full advantage of this one."

"Who's this Potelle and how do you know he shot this arrow?"

"He's a mercenary. He sells his services to anyone who'll pay his price. He's without an ounce of loyalty to anything but gold, but he's very good at what he does. And he marks his arrows.

"Why would he mark his arrows?"

"He's proud of his work and he has no fear of being known. Actually he likes it. It adds to his reputation and raises his price."

"Where do we find him?"

"You don't. I chased him once, a long time ago, over something between us. He escaped to France. I followed him there. Never found him. I heard he'd returned a few years ago. He's very good with a sword, and the best archer I've ever seen, Robin included."

Albert joined us. "I've cleaned it. It's not so bad as it might have been."

I asked, "What do we do now?"

John thought we should stay in the camp for at least a few days, until Robin was a little recovered, then move to the smaller clearing we called Marigold. Opinion was split, but in the end we all agreed that if Tuck was right and the arrow was from the man called Potelle, then Thoren wasn't coming back and we need not fear another attack. At least not anytime soon. Tuck agreed, he said what was wanted, was done

With the arrival of morning we woke to find that John had already left the camp. I'd been up early with him. Tuck came up behind me and asked about Robin. "Sleeping." I told him. And John? "Out. You know John, wants to be sure." Tuck smiled and agreed John was always very careful.

In the evening sitting at the fire we heard the sound of footsteps in the distance moving strongly over the forest floor.

Tuck, "Too loud and too fast to be anyone trying to go unnoticed. Must be John. But, I'll meet whoever it is." He was back shortly with John. It became a night of talk – talk again about what we should do. The sense of safety that had been agreed to yesterday was eroding quickly. Many felt we were vulnerable to another attack and without Robin leading us there was a general concern about being able to do again what we had done two days ago. Robin seemed a little better, he had longer periods when he was awake, but he'd lost a good deal of blood and there was no doubt he needed rest, and time to heal. There were no obvious signs of infection and that was good. We talked. It was Tuck who said it and when he did no one denied it.

"The weather's going to turn cold very fast now. Robin would recover better where it's warm and dry. Indoors."

I asked, "What are you suggesting?"

"Take him to the monastery. The monk's will look after him. The rest disperse. Mingle back into the villages, places where you're not known. Stay there until spring, then meet at Marigold clearing. If someone should come back, find the place empty, they'll think we've given up the dog. That would be good."

"We can't make that kind of decision without Robin!" I said, and it was agreed to wait until Robin was better along. We became extremely diligent and sentinels were placed further out than we had ever felt the need for them to be. And they were doubled in number. We thought the rapidly approaching winter was a great ally, but we also were not going to forget what had nearly happened. The camp slipped back to something like what it had been, but not completely. There was an overhanging sense that something had changed. Of course something had changed. Nothing was the same. Never could be again.

A week passed and Robin's recovery wasn't what we had hoped it would be. He didn't seem to have the same ability to rebound as we had seen in the past. His color remained pale and his face drawn. There was no infection, but it was apparent something wasn't right. Albert had done what he could, and there could be no Parmon this time. By the end of the second week Robin was on his feet, but he was by no means recovered.

His color was better, but not right. He'd lost a good deal of weight.

It was a sad time, the sense of concern had become a sense of dread, almost doom. And the grey weather of an almost fully arrived winter didn't help. In fact, the cold was deeper than usual for that time of year and we all sensed that it would be a bad winter. What made it even worse was that a number of the men had been showing the same paleness that Robin had, and Sean and Harold were the worst of all. In fact, there were days when Sean was too weak to do much of anything. To call it a depressed time would be far less than the truth.

It was Robin who called us all together and shocked us with his proposal. It was basically the same as what Tuck had suggested. He spoke about our comradeship and how it would survive the winter, and how, when the spring returned, we would resume our life together in the forest. He said he needed time and warmth to finish his recovery and that he was concerned the early severity of the weather was taking its toll on many of us. I listened and I believed some of it. He certainly could do with the indoors. And certainly there were others who could benefit from the same thing. But what he avoided saying and what no one else seemed eager to talk about was the difference in him and the others. The obvious reluctance of his recovery. The general poor health of so many. It was blamed on the winter, but we had spent all the winters before without problems. Men had been wounded before and the winter had never been something we had run from. It was more than the winter. I hated everything that was happening. I hated the obvious and inescapable truth that a great blow had been dealt, and it was not from what had happened to Robin. It was something else, a feeling, or rather a lack of a feeling. There was something missing. Something had gone away, disappeared in the night, vanished. Abandoned us like a treacherous companion who no longer had use for us. There was nothing about the camp that was like before. And I sensed something else - that Robin was filled with guilt, haunted by the prospect that we were no longer safe and he was the one who had put us in danger. In the end, the decision, because it had come from him, was accepted. We would meld quietly back into the villages, Nottingham, Edmonton, Stillwater, wherever we could. Wait until the upcoming winter was over, then meet again. Robin would go to the Monastery at Barnwell and remain for the winter. In the spring, on the first of April, we would meet at Marigold clearing. There was a strange sense of foreboding about the future, you could see it on every face. A great sense of confusion and loss. I realized how much no one had ever considered the future would be anything but Sherwood. Maybe that had never been a realistic belief, but it was their belief and having it rattled as it now was, disjointed them, made them more than uneasy.

Robin had Gregory distribute the future gold. Everyone received an equal share. It was good for them to have it, they would need it over the upcoming months.

There was little to pack, and over the next few days we talked, said goodbye and at different times and in different ways the pairs set off in the gloomy, shadowed, sullen air of approaching winter. Some to the villages, some even as far as London where they felt it would be easier to find a quiet anonymity and await the spring, others, I don't know where.

John, myself, Robin, Tuck, and Marion made east, for the Monastery.

I'd be lying to you if I said I believed we would ever return to Sherwood. I didn't. There was an overwhelming finality in the goodbyes. A great and a sad portent that we had made our last fight, eaten our last meal, laughed our last laugh in the woods. No one said anything of the kind, but I could feel it. I don't know what made me so certain. Others might have said I was wishing it, but that wasn't the case. It was deeper than that, much deeper and much more ominous.

****

When we reached the monastery the intense cold of winter had enveloped the land. The promise of an unusually harsh season was proving correct. The sight of the monastery comfortably nestled in a small valley between softly rolling hills east of Nottinghamshire, with smoke curling dusty white from the fires burning inside its stone walls was a welcome sight.

The monastery was built not so long ago, and it remains well kept and pleasant, but, like all stone buildings, moist and dank in the chill of winter unless a fire is stoked. The monks are pleasant, not unduly obdurate, and were cordial to us – due in no small part to Tuck having been raised there. We concealed the identity of Robin - it seemed best to do so, there was nothing to benefit anyone by making him known, but I don't know if we were successful. Probably not, the monks were not fools. But I don't think it mattered.

The western section being entirely vacant, was left to us and it was there, in the fire warm rooms, that we set ourselves. There were five bedchambers, and a moderately sized central room. Each room had a fire, small, but still capable of taking the chill out of a cool, damp winter night.

Robin used a cane to limp into the monastery, still pale and gaunt, not having gained back any of the weight he'd lost. But his spirits were good and all but myself had confidence that he would make a fine recovery over the winter. I concealed my distrust as best I could and hoped no one would see what I was truly feeling. But when I looked at Marion, saw what was in her eyes, I knew she knew things she wasn't saying. I'd come to the undeniable realization that the health and future of this man was of significant importance to her, and sensed that her future had little meaning if it were not in some way tied to him.

The first days were calm and peaceful, Robin rested, the monks provided plenty of food and drink, and Robin seemed prepared to fully recover. He did develop a fever several days after arriving but it subsided quickly and as he grew stronger everyone seemed anxious to put the past months behind them. Truthfully, as much as I'd come to regard Sherwood as my home and protector, it was not unwelcome to spend a season, especially the winter season, indoors, in warm rooms, fed without need, sleeping above the ground.

Of course the same didn't apply to Tuck, who was often preoccupied to the point of being sullen. I thought I knew what troubled him, and so did John, and we talked about it, agreeing there was time enough for that in the future - for now, it was best to let it go. But Tuck couldn't let it go. On more than one occasion I watched him watching Robin. Tuck's eyes cold at the profile, and filled with guilt, as if he were at fault for what had happened to Robin, for what had happened to all of us. The day came when he turned to see me staring at him and stalked out of the room, motioning me to follow. We went to the courtyard, it was cold and windy, he seemed oblivious to the weather. He said it was his fault because he'd known what Parmon would do and should have killed him when we took him out of the forest. I said it wasn't his fault anymore than it was the fault of anyone else. He said he was the one, the only one. He turned a cold eye on me, "Would you have stopped me?" I laughed, even if I wanted to I couldn't have. I told him so. He laughed too, said I was right and that was all the more reason he blamed himself for not doing it. He asked me to imagine what might now be our situation had he done it. I shrugged, his body shook – violently – He shouted, "None of this, would have happened. None of it!"

Several days later John announced he was going to Nottingham to spend the winter with Martha. Robin appeared happy about it. We would miss him, but it was good and right for him to go. A week later it was my turn. I told Robin I was going to Edmonton. I would spend the winter, try to look up an old friend. He laughed, joked that I had certainly waited long enough. I said I'd return in April.

"Good, go. You've earned your own time."

Before leaving I asked Tuck what he was going to do, stay or go. He said he had business in Shockwell. I knew what he meant. I offered to accompany him, Shockwell was on the way to Edmonton. He asked if I was sure I wanted that. I said yes. "You know the purpose?" I said yes. "And you're committed to it?" I said I wasn't going because I was committed to it, I was going as his friend and I would be watching behind him while he was watching in front. He laughed, said I was a true friend and welcomed my company. I have never forgotten those words because there was no man I'd ever known who would not consider it an honor to be called a friend by Tuck.

We set off on a bright, chilly morning, with little wind. It was nearly a day's walk and we both wanted to reach Shockwell before the sun set. We made good time, said little all the way. There was little to say. Tuck would do what Tuck always did, act - and I'd do what I always did, try to help wherever I could, knowing myself to be not much of a warrior.

We entered the inn and sat at a table behind which the owner was wiping a cup with a dirty cloth, moving rings of filth into new shapes, removing none of them. Only slowly did he look at us. He asked our purpose. His manner wasn't pleasant, but then it wasn't a pleasant place. We asked for wine. He was a stout man, with a large belly, and small, protruding eyes. He put down the cup he was cleaning and poured the ale. I watched the dirt swirls sink into the liquid and then surface and roll incoherently around the edges. I glanced at Tuck, he didn't seem to care very much about the ale. He dropped a farthing on the table. I remember how it clinked on the wood with a hollow sound. It gave me a pause. There was nothing about what we were doing, what was happening, that spoke of anything but bad and I couldn't escape the feeling that the man knew why we were here - of course that was impossible.

There were two men at a small crooked table and another leaning against the far wall, talking to a woman. He was running a hand up and down her thigh. She seemed disinterested. Tuck caught her eye and she managed a half smile. I wondered if they knew each other. Tuck picked up his cup and went to a vacant table in the corner of the room, opposite the men and the woman. I followed and we sat on a bench that groaned under our weight. Tuck took his first drink of the ale and spit it on the floor. I watched it gather itself into a small circle. He cursed the innkeeper and the inn and then we sat quietly and drank it, bad as it was. When his cup was empty Tuck rose and walked to the table where the owner was still running the same dirty rag around the inside of another cup.

"More ale less dirt this time." The owner didn't look up, he just filled the cup. Tuck dropped a farthing on the table. The sensation was even stronger now that the man knew us and our intentions. Then there was a sharp sound, like the crack of a whip. We looked in the direction of the sound. The hand of the woman was raised a second time, but it wasn't necessary, the man had backed away and she called after him, cursing. I found her choice of words amusing, and slightly hypocritical. She saw that we had been watching and sauntered over to our table. Standing in front of Tuck she said "That pig, always trying." She had a missing tooth and several rotting ones, which contrasted with her face which wasn't unattractive, though dirty and unkempt. She seemed one of those women who was drifting into age far more quickly than her years. She was lean, with large breasts, and her hands were coated with a heavy layer of dirt. I suspected by day she worked the fields. She asked Tuck where he was going and he told her it was none of her business. She said she could offer a warm cottage and a bed with "fresh straw, and blankets." Tuck shook his head. She persisted, saying she had stew in a pot. She glanced at me and said I was also welcome. Tuck told her to go away. She seemed insulted, but didn't move. He told her again in that voice of his that couldn't be mistaken for anything but dangerous. She sneered, began to move away, turned and asked if he were sure. He said he was.

The door of the tavern opened and two men came in, loudly. They were dirty from the fields. The woman followed them with her eyes, then with her body, approaching them as soon as they sat. They seemed willing to allow her, and soon the three of them were talking and laughing.

We could hear most of the conversation, it was bawdy, often explicitly descriptive of what the men were interested in. More than once she glanced at us as if to tell us we had made a mistake in rejecting her. We finished our ale. It was near the time to make our visit to Parmon. The door of the tavern opened again, a woman entered. I thought I saw recognition in Tucks eyes. When she saw us she spent a moment staring at him, ignoring me. He returned her look. She came toward us. Tuck told me to say nothing. From the conversation, which went as follows, it was obvious to me that he knew her.

"What are you doing here?" She spoke in a whisper, looking around the room quickly.

"None of your business."

"No need to be nasty."

"What new news in Shockwell?"

"News?"

"Yes, news!"

"They say there was trouble in Sherwood."

"What kind of trouble?"

"I don't know, just trouble."

Tuck looked away, she took a seat next to him, closely.

"Have you been with Parmon lately?"

"What do you care?"

"I didn't say I cared."

"Then why ask?"

"I'm sorry I did."

"He gives me things."

"Does he?"

"Yes."

"And that makes him better?"

"Better than what?"

"Better than a pig?"

"Better than someone who doesn't give me anything. You never gave me anything."

"No, I didn't. So what does he give you?"

"He gives me things that'll keep me young."

"You don't really believe that do you?"

"Believe what?"

"That he can make you stay young longer?"

"Maybe...anyway, what harm does it do? If it doesn't work it does no harm."

"Are you sure of that?"

"What does that mean?"

"Do you know what he puts in those vials? Does he even know what he puts in those vials? Does he know what they might really do?"

"He's been to Constantinople. To the East. He speaks Greek and he knows secrets. How do you know what Parmon can do? You're not a physician."

"What else does he know?"

"What do you mean?"

Tuck suddenly reached into the pocket of her apron and pulled out a purse near to bursting. Her face whitened. "Where did you get this money?"

"What money?" It enraged Tuck. He dropped the purse to the table and struck her across the face. Her lip broke and a small trickle of blood ran down her chin. I reached for his arm, he turned on me. His eyes made me sit back. The owner of the inn shouted at him, something about fighting inside his place. One of the men at the other side of the room rose, I saw him pull a dagger from his belt. Tuck rose and drew his sword. "Do you know me?" It was addressed to everyone. There was no response, "My name is Tuck." The innkeeper took several steps back. The man who had drawn his dagger put it back in his belt and took his seat, turning his back to us. Tuck sat, but didn't sheath the sword. She wiped her lip.

"What's the matter with you! I didn't do anything to deserve that!"

"He gave you the money!" It was very clear she wanted to lie, very clear she knew that she couldn't. And very clear to me why we had come to this particular inn. There were things Tuck knew about her and Parmon. She didn't answer, he repeated what he'd said. She said,

"Yes."

"For what?"

"You know for what."

"Liar!" He slapped her again, a small cut broke over her left cheek, it trickled blood. She was white and began shaking.

"You were a part of it from the beginning. You were there the night we took him." She didn't respond. "You knew, you were part of it!"

"Part of what?" The trembling increased. I thought she might shake herself into pieces. He leaned close to her and whispered in her ear.

"No!" She shouted, jumping to her feet.

"Don't lie to me Jesse! If you want to live, don't lie to me!"

"No. No. I had no idea until it was done. I found out after it was done!"

"And then you used it to make him pay!"

"I saw no harm in it. It was already done, I had nothing to do with it happening."

"How did you find out?"

"He was drunk, half asleep, he said some things, I fed him more of me and more liquor and he talked. He was proud of it. Then he passed out. The next day I told him I knew. He said I was lying, that he had nothing to do with what happened. I told him I'd find a way to get to someone in Sherwood. He dragged me to his cabin, promised me anything, any potion. I wanted gold. He gave it and then said if I broke my promise he'd say I was in league with him from the beginning."

Tuck sheathed his sword, rose, took her by the arm and dragged her out, motioning me to follow. I wasn't sure exactly what he was going to do to her, but I was certain of what he would do to Parmon.

We stood in front of the cottage of the alchemist. In the light of a three quarter moon, the house seemed more decrepit, more obtuse than the first time we had been there. It seemed to lean to the left. The windows seemed smaller, deeper, like tunnels. Tuck banged away at the door. I could hear the sound echoing in the cottage like a broken bell, heavy, cordless. No answer. Tuck drew his sword and used the hilt. Then a voice, calling through the door, muffled, confused, possibly just wakened by the knocking.

"Who is it?"

"Tuck."

"Tuck?"

"Yes."

No response.

Several more seconds passed, Tuck was beyond impatience. He smashed the door again with the hilt of the sword. The voice again. No mistaking that it was full of fear.

"What do you want Tuck?"

"I need help. I have sick men. Very sick. Open the door!"

"I can't, I'm busy."

"Open it, or I'll take it down!"

Silence. We waited. As he was about to strike the door with his shoulder it opened slightly, slowly on rusted hinges. Parmon stuck his nose through the tiny opening he'd made.

"What do you want?"

"I told you, I want medicine."

"Now, in the middle of the night?"

"Illness doesn't keep track of the time."

"I told you I'm busy."

Tuck pushed the door quickly, viciously back and it knocked the skinny man to the hard dirt floor. He pulled the reluctant Jesse inside with him, motioned me to follow, and closed the door. He flung the girl forward with a whip like motion of his arm, and she flew like a weed, tripping over Parmon and falling to the ground. I felt that I was no longer a living breathing person, no longer capable of my own thoughts, my own actions. I was a statue, a puppet, I'd do what I was told to do and I'd witness what would happen and it would be emblazoned forever in my brain. My breath was even, but cold. Neither the fallen Parmon, nor Jesse had attempted to rise.

"Get up!" Parmon rose on shaky legs, trembling with concern. Jesse remained on the dirt, not knowing what to do. "I said get up." She rose slowly. And then they were two, standing before Tuck, his eyes blazing like red hot coals in the cottage that was lit only by a candle that sat on a table in the middle of the room. He took in everything, and when satisfied that there was nothing to concern him he shouted at Parmon, "You pig! You sold us to the sheriff." I watched Parmon's lips move, but no sound came out. "You sold us for money, like cattle for slaughter. But you were stupid. You had no idea about us. And you lost your gamble. Robin Hood is alive, Little John, Scarlett, me, and all the others. But you know that, don't you!" He went to Parmon and shook him, he vibrated like a skeleton strung together with wire. "Did you know about Potelle?" Parmon shook his head and asked who was Potelle. Tuck screamed at him, "Don't play me for a fool! Did you know about him being sent to follow Thoren?" Parmon shook his head. I thought he was telling the truth. I don't know what Tuck thought. He released his grip and Parmon fell back. He paced before him and the girl. Then, striking the floor with the tip of his sword he shouted, "We paid you what you asked. The sheriff paid you more. Now you have to pay what we ask." Parmon was white, his piano playing hands didn't move. The deep set eyes were no longer deep set – they bulged. He stared at Tuck's sword.

"What are you going to do?"

"Kill you."

"No!"

Parmon found the sudden strength to turn and run to the door of his laboratory. Tuck smiled as he watched the petrified man reach for the keys that always dangled from his neck. He fumbled hopelessly, trying to unlock the door, and finally in a burst of uncontrolled hysteria he managed to open the lock and push back the door. Tuck's back was to me, but I could hear him laughing. Parmon was now in the room and had slammed the door behind him, locking it from the inside. Tuck took two steps to Jesse, grabbed her by the arm, pulled her to her feet and dragged her to the door of the laboratory. He flung her to his right against the wall, she hit it solidly, her head came off the wall with a heavy sound and she slumped to the ground like a rag. I shouted to him that it wasn't right to kill her. She hadn't betrayed us. He ignored me, raised his sword and smashed it against the door. Again, again. The door splintered and wood flew across the room. He raised a foot and pushed against it - it gave way and fell inward - he stormed into the room. I could see Parmon standing behind a table filled with bottles and vials and twisting, spiraling pieces of glass of unusual colors. He was ghastly pale and trembling. Tuck moved toward him, stopped, turned and said, "Watch her!" Then he continued toward Parmon, who had picked up a vial of amber liquid. He threw it. Tuck dodged the vial and it flew past my face. It smashed against the wall behind me foaming and hissing as it ate into the stone. Then another bottle. Again past Tuck and me and into the door behind us. Parmon ran to the far corner of the room, and as he ran, his flailing arms smashed into a large bottle of clear liquid. The bottle broke and the liquid splashed on the wooden table top, over the floor and into the air. The splattering of it hit Parmon on the face, on the neck, the arms, the chest, the shoulders, and his skin set to seething and smoking like it had been set afire by an unseen torch. He began to wail. "Help me! Help me Tuck! I'll give you anything you want! Help me, don't do it, don't! I have gold! Lot's of gold! You can have it all. All of it! Every piece! Please help me, spare me! Please!" I have never heard a man beg for his life, before or since, in the voice and with the fear that Parmon begged. Even now I can hear him and even now I shiver at the sound of it in my mind. I will never forget it, I will never be able to expel it. It's a part of me – of what I am, what I was then. If I were Tuck I couldn't have done it. I knew it then and I know it even more now. I wanted to say something that might make him stop. I remembered our conversation in the woods when he'd asked me if I would have tried to stop him. But it was too far gone now, too much had taken place, too many had died. The sword moved quickly and true.

Parmon was gone.

Tuck turned to me. Jesse lay on the ground, still dazed from the shock and the pain in her head. He stood above her. I said his name in almost a whisper. He looked at me. I wanted to ask for her life. The words didn't come, I hoped my eyes were speaking for me. She was staring up at him, pleading. I said his name again, louder. With Parmon I'd been helpless and had left it to him, but this, the girl, seemed so wrong that if I let it go I was sure I'd be damned for the rest of my life and then welcomed into the hottest fires of hell. He kept looking between us. At her, then at me. I shook my head. She was pleading for her life between sobs. He answered her pleas by telling her she'd done wrong – it was no matter that the money had been taken after it had been done. He told her he couldn't let her go unpunished. She begged him to let her live. He moved the sword to his left hand and brought the other, with its heavy glove and beaded metal points, against her face with an awful force. I heard an ugly sound and knew he'd broken her cheek. Blood poured from the wound and flowed over her chin and onto her chest. She screamed in pain. I knew then he wasn't going to kill her - I knew what his intent was. He'd branded her. Her face, would always bear the scar of what she'd done. He bent low over her and tore a piece of cloth from her dress. He pushed it into her hand, and moved the hand over the bleeding. He pulled her to her feet and told her to go. She was too frightened, too much in shock to move. He took her by the arms, gently now, and walked her to the door of the cottage, removed the bolt and moved her into the cold night air. He held her up for several minutes, letting the air revive her, and letting her mind realize it was over. He told her again to go. "Go, and get help for your face." She looked up at him and thanked him for sparing her. I could see how painful it was for her to speak. He asked her if she knew where Parmon kept his money. She motioned to the back room where Parmon lay and then with halting words said "a bag behind the cupboard." He told her to wait, motioned for me to help her. I put an arm around her. She looked into the sky and the dark. She kept the piece of cloth pressed against her cheek. I saw tears in her eyes, they fell and mingled with the blood, but no sound came from her. Tuck reappeared. He handed her a bag and told her it contained a large sum of money. He instructed her to see that it was divided. Half she could keep. The other half she was to deliver to the monastery at Barnwell. Then he handed her a small, folded and sealed, piece of parchment. Deliver it and the money, herself, he said, entrust it to no one else. She nodded her head. He seemed to know she would see to it. He said goodbye and told her to leave. As she began to move off, unsteadily, weaving as one does when drunk, he said to me, "Pen, my friend, this is goodbye for us too." And before I could say anything he was off, in the dark, quickly. As he moved through the low grass at the edge of the village his feet made little noise, other than a soft whoosh, whoosh. My eyes moved between his disappearing form and that of the girl, she was weaving and I knew it was hard for her to keep afoot, I started toward her but then it struck me with all the force of that sword he wielded so well. Perhaps I hesitated too long. The thought has plagued me ever since that night. But the truth is that there would have been nothing I could have done except to anger him. When I was near to the bank I could see him in the moonlight, waist high in the water. He turned to the sound of my racing through the reeds. He put up a hand and waved at me, first to wave me off, then to wave goodbye and then I saw the vial in his hand. He pulled the cork, put the vial to his mouth swallowed it quickly, and was gone, under the water. I ran like a madman, jumped into the river and thrashed my way to where he'd been but couldn't find him.

It had happened so quickly, but so slowly. I wasn't even sure if it had happened – was Parmon dead - had there been a girl - had I been there, or anywhere. Had there been a Tuck, a Sherwood, a life outside the life of reality. Had I been dreaming and was all this nothing? Was there ever a Robin Hood and had I ever stumbled into the woods in fear of my life? It was all dream-like and hazy. It seemed I had been somewhere far away and had come back to where I now was and would never be able to reconcile the two places. Then there was the chill of the cold water and I made my way out of it, took only a few steps onto the land and fell to the ground. I don't know how long it was before I rose and began to make my way. I know that when I did, it was still dark, but the darkness didn't last very long before the sun began to break the horizon. I was cold, and wet, but it all seemed to be of little consequence. What stood before my mind was that Sherwood was gone, Tuck was gone and even if April did arrive, I knew my life would never again be what it had been, and in a sad way and what I knew was weakness, I felt very sorry for myself. And I couldn't help the emptiness of knowing Tuck was no longer in the world. Angry, hostile, dangerous Tuck – missing him was hard and definite.

There remains only one more thing for me to tell, and it concerns the diary of Parmon.

Earlier I mentioned that Parmon kept a diary. After sitting for some time in the dark I thought of the diary. I wondered what it might have to say about the Sheriff, Thoren and the giving up of the secret of the camp. How had he been able to know it with a hood over his face. I made a quick dash back to his cabin before taking the road toward Nottingham. I scrambled amongst the mess and found it. I had no interest in any of it save those entries that might shed more light on what I wanted to know. A good deal of it had been damaged and made unreadable by the splashing of all those vials and pots, but there were pages intact that were dated very recently. I stuffed all of it into my pocket and left. I include below just the words you should read, they are sufficient to give the truth about the Sheriff and Potelle.

Today I wait for Jesse. Pretty girl. I look forward to her. She is obliging. I like her skin. Too many of them are too old and wrinkled or dry from the sun and the wind. She's soft. And the prettiest yet.

Jesse is gone, yesterday night. What a time! She wants the potion that will keep her young! I gave it to her. She deserves it. The younger she stays the more I'll enjoy being with her. I believe she spends time with that Tuck. The wild man with the big sword. He's crazy, I'm sure of that. Crazy wounded in the head and heart. I have a suspicion he spends time with the perverts in the forest. I would like to know that for sure. There must be money to be made from them.

I'm back from the forest. Back from the camp. They took me there to fix Robin Hood. A bad wound from a dirty tusk. I was, in the beginning at my wits end. I knew if I wasn't successful, they would kill me. They think they are so smart! So clever! In reality they are stupid and so full of themselves! Perverts all, except a few, and Marion, a beauty. What I would like to do to her! I took my position several times each night, it is the first time I have used the instrument they gave me in Constantinople. I'm hoping it works.

My calculations are done. I need to test them. I will do so tomorrow night. The moon will be new and there will be very little light and they do not post sentries at night. Jesse will be here soon. I welcome that body to my bed.

I was right! The camp is where I calculated it to be. This will be very saleable information.

Sold! Sold! The Sheriff is happy, I'm happy! Much more than I thought he would pay. The fat little fool. I would have sold for half!

I will go tomorrow on the journey. More than three days, but I have a feeling it will be worth the effort. She is rich, and she must want to know how to get to him.

She is a brutal woman! I would not want her against me. She paid well to know where he was. She asked me about a man named Potelle. I know nothing of him, and told her so. She wasn't happy about that. I'm home now and the wife of that merchant will be around soon. A little worn, but still she gives well of herself.

It was strange to know that it was Goneril who had arranged for Potelle to follow Thoren and kill Robin. Given what I knew of her and what others said, it should not have been a surprise, but still, it was. A hard woman. Evil, without a conscience. She nearly succeeded in killing him. Robin never knew who had sent Potelle. Neither did anyone else. I have never told anyone.

Some time later, after I had left Robin and Marion at the monastery, I wrote him a note. I'd heard about the others, how sick they all were. I was glad I wasn't. I wondered why. I had no answer to it, but if something is right, leave it alone. I gave the note to Scarlett and asked that he deliver it to Robin.

What was in it is not important. Something between Robin and myself. Something I knew he would understand and something I hoped he would cherish, take with him to wherever he was going – maybe tell Tuck about it when they met again. I'd like to tell you that it was a note of goodbye, or encouragement or some such other useless sentiment that people are consumed with when they realize that the end of something is about to occur and they suddenly become aware of all the things they should have done, should have said, should have been. But it wasn't a note like that at all, because what I had done up to that point, all I had been, could not be changed. I'd even come to know that there was no reason to regret what had happened to Tuck. It wasn't my place, my duty, my destiny to change that. Tuck was to do what Tuck was to do and I was just a player in the drama, an actor if you will, on the same stage, playing my part, and stepping out of that part was impossible. So, the note wasn't, couldn't have been one of those sad and lonely confessions, or worse yet, one of those deeply stirring anthems. It was just a simple thing I wanted to say, a simple note from a simple man to a legend. In the years that have passed I have often smiled over the memories of those days and just as often have been able to know beyond a shadow of any doubt that I have nothing to regret, no blame to place and no pity to ask for. Time will not care about me. History will place no markers on my grave. There will be no songs written that include me. I will pass into the great masses of the anonymous. Even these pages will not have any great effect on my posterity because I have no posterity. Robin Hood has posterity because he was the first and the best of those who tried so diligently to find a way to live in a world that had no compassion for him and in so doing had given so many others a place to do the same.

Whatever else need be said will be done by Marion because the last of it, the whole last of it, is known by her. And now it will be known by you.

When I have all the parts I will put them in a safe place. Someplace where I know they will remain for a very long time, unseen, unknown. But a place that will eventually see the light of day, and when that happens I hope they are found by someone with courage. The courage of a Robin Hood.

There is really nothing else I can say, or need to. But I assume, if you could, you would have questions of me. I believe I know what some of them would be. Unfortunately I will not be there to answer them. If I were, I might respond with questions of my own.

I might ask have you ever walked Cadbury Road with Robin Hood and Little John? Have you ever had Tuck look you in the eye and call you a friend? Have you ever seen Cally and Marion tend the wounds of men who were called queer? Have you ever seen them in Marigold clearing, sitting calmly while they await their fate? Have you ever been alone in the great dark forest when the only friend you had was just as frightened as yourself? Have you ever stared down the long, cold blade of a broadsword and wondered why? Have you ever seen Parmon play the piano in the sky with fingers of doom? Have you ever seen a woman weep because the man she loved had smashed her face and changed her soul forever? Have you ever seen a man wither and die on the vine while the sun was still high and his life should have been just beginning? Have you ever known that you could never live your life in the clear open light of day because the clear open light of day was denied to you upon your birth? Have you ever seen the wealthy whine and the poor laugh? Have you ever said goodbye to courage beyond compare and craved a love that never dies? Have you ever done, seen, been any of this? The forest has seen it all. The forest held it, then gave it back so that it might die and be reborn as a legend. I know this to be fact, because I was there.

So, I have told you what it is I set out to tell you. I don't believe I've embellished it at all. Everything happened as I put it down. What you choose to make of it thus far is, of course, your business. My business was to say it and hopefully clear the air and put to rest all the insane versions of it that paint a picture, not of a real man that could really exist, but a storybook character that has little foundation in reality. The Robin Hood I knew was real. And he was a man worth knowing. He had faults, he had demons, and he had a lot of friends. Good men who would have, and in some cases, did lay down their lives for him.

I have only now to give you what Marion has said and having given it, wish you a good day.

Marion:

Not so many knew where I'd been all those years after it was over. And in France, those who did know didn't care. At least not in the way they would have in England because in France what had been heard of Robin Hood was small and, at the time I first went there, not so great a tale as it became. And that was good because when I first arrived in France I was a defeated and tired woman, trying to forget what had happened and how much it had crushed my spirit. It took many years before I was able to face it well enough to allow it into my life. It was a very long time, nearly thirty years when he came to me and asked me if I'd write it down. He said he'd already been to Thoren and he'd agreed. I asked him why he wanted me to write it. He said there was already growing a great legend in England and he was sure it would continue to grow and spread and what was being said was completely wrong. It was, he said, a horrible lie meant to hide the truth about what Sherwood had been, and if there was going to be anything remembered, it should be the truth. I asked him why me? He was there from the very beginning, before I was. He said he wasn't there at the end, and not during all those last months when I was with Robin and it was just the two of us. I asked him about Thoren and he said he needed Thoren because he was the only one who knew how the attack had been put together, except for the Sheriff and Parmon, both of whom were dead. I told him I'd consider it, but I would not guarantee it. I didn't know if I could revisit it in the detail he wanted. I'd learned to accept it, even make it part of me, but to write it down, all of it, was something I wasn't sure I could do. He said it was my decision but if I'd ever loved Robin, then it was my duty to put down the truth. He left for England, saying he would return in a year. "I'm old now Marion. If this is to be done, it must be done soon." I held him close, he was such a good man. Two weeks later I began. At first it was difficult, not the memory of it - that was all very clear, I could see it in my mind as if it were happening right before me, now. I could remember the conversations, word for word, clear and precise. It was difficult because it became a re-living of it. Several times I stopped for days on end because of that. But, in the end, I did it. As much – I believe – for myself as for making the truth of it known. And having done it, I have come to feel that it was important to do, and that I have made Robin whole again, complete, as vibrant in death as he was in life. That feels very, very good. Many times since putting it down I have sensed him around me and many times I have had the sensation he is very happy that I have told it the way it was.

And I have heard from Pen. He crosses the channel next week. I will give this to him. I know he will be happy to have it.

What follows, what I have put down, is the truth of Robin and Marion.

****

I was then a young woman called Marion. I had been a ward of the court of Richard before he left for the crusades. With his departure I became answerable to Prince John. I don't speak arrogantly when I say that my beauty had been remarked upon and was frequently spoken of in the court. As much as it was true, I took no great personal pride in it. It wasn't an achievement of mine, it was an accident of birth. I saw no reason to suppose it made me any better than any other woman. But apparently Prince John felt otherwise, or perhaps he just became curious. He had me brought to the summer castle, he could that. He could do anything he wished, Richard was fighting the crusades, and so he ruled without interference. In fact, it was said that John would like nothing better than to have Richard never return. Once there, and having laid eyes on me, he wasted no time in making advances, which I resisted. He would not give up. It became very uncomfortable. He wasn't a handsome man, neither in form or manner. In fact I found him rather course, sometimes rude. Even as a king there was nothing about him or his power as a king, that interested me. Several weeks passed and then what I saw as being inevitable, happened. He told me he had the power - the right - to take what he wanted and said it would be so much better, so much more to my benefit if I didn't force him to exercise his power over me. So much more pleasant and beneficial to me if I acted of my own free will. He made great promises about the future. I believed none of them and even if I did, I had no interest in a future filled with material things if it was to be spent with a man like him. I told him so. He tried very hard to hold his temper. I could see his hands trembling. John wasn't a man to take rejection. He reiterated his demands and his promises, as if in doing so something would change my mind. I found it humorous and couldn't hold back a smile. He saw the smile for what it was. He became even more troubled. I became worried. I told him that if he did anything untoward, when Richard returned he would be a sorry man. He went from anger to rage, which was often the case when his brother's name was used as a caution to him. He told me that his brother would not care what happened to me. I said I doubted that. And reminded him that my father was well regarded in my homeland of France. He laughed made some disgusting joke about the French and told me I need learn better manners. I told him my manners were perfectly fine and it was certainly he who needed counseling in the art of courtly behavior. He couldn't deal with the fact that I didn't seem to be afraid of him. Of course I was afraid of him. He had the power to do as he wished, but my father had taught me that showing fear was something to be avoided in persons wishing to control their own destiny.

There was going to be no denying him, I was sure of that, and it finally came to a head, when he entered my private rooms uninvited. I ordered him out – he laughed. He came toward me and I told him I'd never submit willingly to him. He said that willingly or not he would have his way. I threatened him with exposure to the church and he went wild with laughter. "The Church? Why would I be afraid of the Church? I rule England. My brother fights to free their holy land. Their indebtedness to our family, and our money is endless. The Church!"

"Take me then, do what you want, but you'll do it alone!" He came to me and tried to kiss me. I resisted, or rather I turned my face from him. He pulled it back. He had ugly lips, fat, distorted, he put them against me and forced my mouth open. I began to feel sick to my stomach. He tore my dress, then my bodice, and tossed me onto the bed. Then he was on top of me, fondling. I thought of the dagger that resided by my bed, but would not let him drive me to such a crime. I stared at the ceiling, determined to let him do as he wished without any more fighting. Better to have it over with than to risk being beaten in addition. That angered him. He shouted some oath I didn't understand. It seemed he couldn't accept my indifference, then in a frenzied rage he jumped to his feet and screamed at me. I don't recall what he said, perhaps he said nothing, perhaps it was just a wild roar of incoherent anger. Nonetheless I didn't move. I made no attempt to cover myself. He stopped the railing and stared at me. Then he hit me, several times. It was hard and awful and I thought he'd broken my face. I felt faint, the room began to spin. I could taste the warmth of blood in my mouth. I lost consciousness.

When I awoke I was on my bed. Two ladies in waiting stood, one on either side. They told me to lie still, it was over. I drifted in and out of sleep for I don't know how long. I remember that there were two men, one of whom I recognized as a physician of the court tending to me, but I was never able to remain conscious for very long. When they told me it had been three days I wasn't surprised, nor did I care. I asked about my face, my cheek throbbed. One of the women said that it was badly injured but that the healing had already begun and there would be no damage to my beauty. My beauty! They all seemed so concerned about my beauty! I tried to laugh, it hurt too much. In my mind I cursed my beauty and cursed that wicked man.

It was during my recovery that I decided I must leave the castle, leave England. I sent letters to my father, but heard nothing in return. I asked one of those who had attended me in the first days of the injury and she was reluctant to speak about it. I prodded. She checked every corner of the room then whispered in my ear that no letters ever reached my father, and, her voice grew even lower, "I fear that there are plans afoot to put you in the tower." There was little left to choice. I was sure John was arrogant enough to ignore anything when it came to meting out punishment he felt was due. I had a purse filled with gold coin. I considered every option I could think of for several days. I saw no alternative but to take the most desperate steps. John wasn't a man prone to compassion or leniency and I'd wronged his manhood in a way he wasn't going to forgive, far from it. Two days later I slipped out of the castle in the darkest part of the night, determined to make my way to the coast and then back to France. It was a foolish and stupid thing to do. The chance of being successful was nigh to none, but I couldn't risk staying any longer, not after what I'd been told about the tower. People who went into the tower rarely came out, and if they did it was in a pine box. It seemed better to die running, hunted down by John's men than to languish away in the tower, or be killed.

The summer castle was just outside of Nottingham. I spent the night in the barn of a farmer and was up at dawn before I could be discovered. I found my way to the main road from Nottingham and then to the great highway, and stopped the first wagon I saw. I offered money to take me south. The man seemed reluctant at first, but when I put the gold pieces in his hand his attitude changed. I worried he might be the kind of man who would do me harm because he'd seen the purse from which I'd taken the money, but I had a dagger and I was determined to use it at any hint of treachery. We began our journey south without incident. We moved along the edge of Sherwood Forest on the road known as Broadmore Way, a wide, straight road that would take us to the great highway that ran to London. The man had agreed to take me as far as Carstock, which he said we would make by dusk. He said there was a large inn, and carriages to London stopped there. As we traveled I glanced frequently back to the castle, it was comforting to see it slipping farther and farther away. About half an hour into our journey I saw them, or rather the dust they were driving into the air. I knew immediately he'd sent them after me. I screamed at the driver to urge on his horse and he said that he could go no faster, the horses simply couldn't be worked any harder than he was working them. I demanded more speed, offered him more money, and it was then that his face changed. He took a long look at me, up and down in a way he'd not done before. I sensed he was looking for clues about me. I had not told him anything when I'd stopped him other than that I needed transport and I could pay my way. And he'd not asked anything other than to see the gold first. Now, there was a morbid curiosity in his eyes. I knew he sensed there was more to my story and perhaps more gold to be made. Suddenly he pulled up the wagon and looked to the road behind us. He saw it too and began to quiz me heavily, not accepting my constant complaint that he had no need to concern himself with anything but moving the wagon ahead, quickly. "Quickly or not, we'll never escape whoever it is that's racing behind us. Racing I'll bet to find you!" I denied that. He shook his head, asked if I were a thief, or a convict. I asked him did I look like either. He was forced to admit I didn't, "But the make of the clothes are not always the make of the person." I assured him he had nothing to worry about. "Nothing to worry about? Then why all the rushing. If whoever it is that's behind us isn't interested in you, all we have to do is pull to the side of the road and let them pass!" He pressed me again and I resisted, knowing that if he knew the truth he would abandon me on the spot. I tried to fabricate another lie, something plausible, halfway through my explanation he grabbed me, then tossed me into the back of the cart, turned it round and began racing toward the dust cloud that was growing ever closer. I knew he would try to save himself and attempt to get more gold by telling them I'd lied to him. We moved like thunder over the hard dirt and although I thought of jumping it seemed like suicide. He whipped the horse on and the men began to form more clearly out of the distance as our separation from them grew less and less. And what was more frightening was that they were dressed in the clothes of the Prince's guard. If the driver had any doubts they were gone. There was no choice. I told myself I'd been foolish, but must now be foolish again if there was to be any chance of saving myself. I took a deep breath and jumped from the cart to the side of the road closest to the forest. I hit the dirt painfully and rolled quickly into the thick grass and then came to rest. He was so fixed on looking toward the approaching horsemen that he didn't see me jump. I dragged myself to my feet. There was a trickle of blood running down my cheek and another running over my left eye. I wiped them away and raced into the woods, glad to be alive and able to move. Within the cover of the oaks I stopped, but then realized my only chance was to lose myself as far into the woods as I could go, as quickly as possible, and not to stop until I could no longer move, or was dead. I ran as I'd never run before and I'm sure that fear fueled me in ways I'd never been fueled before. I don't know how far I'd gone, nor for how long. I did know that the brambles and the lowest of the branches whipped and tugged at me and there were cuts along both arms and scratches on my face that burned, but I kept moving, from a run to a trot, and finally, as exhaustion set in, to a walk, constantly throwing my eyes over my shoulder. I saw no pursuit. It began to become clear to me that horsemen would not have been able to follow through the dense undergrowth and there was no trail in sight that could have led them near me. I was somewhat reassured, but still I kept the pace as best I could. I'd no idea where I was going, nor what would be the result of my race into the woods, I only knew that I couldn't allow myself to be caught. It was when darkness began to shorten my vision that I realized how long I had been in the forest. Hours. I must have traveled a good distance and might stop, rest. I sat on the forest floor and leaned against a tree. Now I saw the reality of the day play itself out in my mind. What I'd done, and the great insanity of where I was. And also the sudden sense of hunger, and thirst. But the hunger and the thirst became second to the fear of what might lurk in the dark of the trees. What animals would be out with the night? I had no choice but to admit to the hopelessness of what I'd done. If I survived the night, what then? I had no idea where to go, what direction was best. I had the thought - that I couldn't put aside - if some hungry animal found me perhaps he'd make short work of it and everything would be over, quickly and finally. Then I remembered the dagger. I pulled it out. I could save the animal the trouble of killing me. I could do that myself and put an end to the entire misery of what my life had become. I wondered if I had the courage for it. Then I heard the noise. Light at first, almost as if it wasn't there. Then again, and I was sure it was there. It grew more insistent and I sat upright. I hoped it would be quick. Then he was there, standing in front of me, and another one. Men, not animals. And the words, "Are you all right?" I couldn't speak. "Are you all right?" I nodded my head. "What are you doing here?" I shook my head. I wanted to speak but the words wouldn't come. "What's your name?" I struggled to say it. One of them offered me his hand. I took it. He told me not to be afraid, they would take me to their camp. There was fire, food, water. They didn't seem like bad men, there was something forgiving about them, something kind. But they were still men, and although my being here was not exactly normal, what were they doing in the forest? But I was tired and wasted and decided I didn't care what they did with me, so long as when they decided to kill me they did it quickly. It had all gone so badly wrong.

One was in front of me, the other behind. They moved with such certainty and seemed to know the woods the way someone would know the roads of a village. Darkness had fallen completely, and it was a long while before I saw the faint light between the trunks. As we moved closer to the light it became a tremendous fire and a clearing and then we entered and I saw dozens of people scattered in groups around that fire. All men, save one woman. As we approached they smiled and appeared curious but asked no questions. The men who had led me in went to a man who seemed to be the leader. Beside him was a giant of a man.

That night is when the beginning of my real life began. It was also when the end of the reason for living began. But at that exact time I knew about neither, I only knew the fire was warm, there was water and food and everyone seemed anxious to help me.

****

I was accepted readily, even before I told them how I'd come to the forest. Cally, who quickly became a great friend did all she could to help settle me down that first night. I assume my appearance suggested I'd gone through a difficult ordeal. The giant, was very gentle and asked me a few questions but nothing about his manner was demanding. When I heard the name Robin Hood, I realized where I was. I was with that band in the forest who were called outlaws, but were also known to me as perverted people who pursued a way of life that was condemned by the Church and the laws of England. My ease began to turn to misgivings. This was certainly no place for me, not as I was. I wondered if I'd gone from the frying pan into the fire. It wasn't long before I saw that Cally sensed my fears and it was she who first asked me the questions about just how I came to be in the forest and from what was I fleeing. It seemed that she expected me to tell her I was running from the same persecution as the others. When she realized from my explanation that was not the case she laughed and held me close. It made me very uncomfortable. I admit now to mistrusting her intentions. Then she said, "Me, Little John, Tuck, Robin, and now you! Robin will have a laugh. He always jokes about us being misfits!" I asked what she meant and she said I was now the fifth. The fifth what I asked.

"The fifth of us that's not here like the rest. Not queer." I wondered that she was so freely using such a word amongst those who could clearly hear our conversation. But there was nothing in her actions, nor those of anyone else that said it was a problem. She said everyone who lived here did so without concern for who they loved or how they loved - it was a family of friends, and no one plagued the other over what she called silly matters. "Little John has Martha, Tuck has every pretty woman who crosses his path and I have…well…I had a husband. He's long passed and I'm in no hurry to find another one. At least not now. Someday, when he gives my heart permission." We talked for a while before the giant she called Little John approached with another man. A handsome man, lithe and taller than most, though not nearly so tall as John. Clean shaven and with long auburn hair. His smile was the warmest I'd ever seen. He bowed and gave his name as Robin Hood, and asked mine. I looked at Cally, she smiled and whispered, "Yes, it's him." I thanked him for his hospitality, he bowed again and said the hospitality was mine so long as I chose to avail myself of it.

I made no decisions about anything the first few days. Too much had happened too fast. And with such a friendly, easy group of companions, there seemed no reason to make hasty decisions. Robin spent a good deal of time with me, talking about my youth, his youth, the fact that we had both spent most of it in ease and comfort. He never said a single word about what I should do, never gave advice. He was very easy to be with and that was very important those first days. Cally too was wonderful. We shared the kinds of conversations only two women can share. We understood the same things, needed the same things, wanted so much of the same. She was here because her husband had been killed trying to defend a woman who had stolen and whom he'd known since he was a child. A woman of a poor family who had gone the way she'd gone because there was no other way. He was a landed man, not wealthy, but comfortable and they had a house outside Nottingham. His land was forfeited and she was stripped of everything. It was Tuck, a friend of her and her husband, who had brought her to the forest.

The men built me a lean-to, close to the fire and the nights and days passed with an ease that surprised me because I was no longer surrounded by the comforts I'd always known and always believed I needed.

Days became weeks and the weeks became a month and with the passing of it I knew I had to make a decision. Cally, like Robin, never suggested I stay, neither did either say I should go. They left me with my own mind and when I finally asked if I could stay for some time, Robin asked how long "some time" might be. I said I had no idea, just that I felt so good about being where I was that I'd let the future set itself. He told me I was welcome so long as I wished, was free to leave if that time ever came. But, if I did, the secrecy of the camp was of such paramount importance that I must swear to never compromise its location or how many lived in it. I agreed. In my heart, at that time, I saw little reason for wanting to go anywhere else, and little need to do so. What awaited me in Nottingham, or any city for that matter? People like the Prince? "So," he said to me, "it's decided." We shook hands on it and he made the announcement to the camp. Little John took me up in his arms and held me high, like I was a feather, while the camp cheered their approval. It was a such a day! The happiness of that moment still exists for me!

****

Life in Sherwood Forest was a new awakening – I'd never lived anywhere but within the walls of a castle. I'd never felt the cold earth beneath my bones, nor the fog wrapping round my body like a damp blanket. I'd never seen the light dart between the trees and find the ground in little sparkling dots reflecting off the early morning wet. I'd never sat with such a large group of happy, laughing people around a tremendous fire eating venison and sharing good humor. Of course it wasn't all easy, there were the things I missed – certain comforts I would not have been adverse to having. But, with every day that passed my marvel at the way the people grappled with adversity with such good spirits and the quiet beauty of the place, made me put aside any small regrets for wealth and walls of stone.

Cally and I took long walks along paths the men had hacked into the forest, stopping at small brooks and creeks where the water ran fast and clear and moss covered rocks gleamed golden green. The sight of a deer racing off in the distance and even the ugly cry of the boar, who could be heard but not seen, brought smiles. Sometimes a small group would make a longer hike and cook by the waterfall we called Private Tears. It was a particularly beautiful place where the men had cut out a small clearing and the sun could blaze down and heat the water while it made that droning sound as it rushed over the edge and into the pool at its base. It was cold in the winter, but in the summer it warmed enough to venture into it. Robin was very fond of that clearing and often he accompanied the groups. It was there, sitting on the soft grass that we began to understand each other more and more. And there that my curiosity began to grow more insistent – asking me why he was alone. True, there were others who had no companion in the camp. John for instance, but he did have Martha and he would leave to be with her every fortnight. Tuck was also alone when with us, but he came and went as a vagabond of the road, and I knew for sure that when he was out of the forest he wasn't alone. And of course Pen, who had been the first to join Robin – and who has asked me to write my history, and became my great friend – and who always said, "some day." Cally I knew the reason for – she seemed incapable of leaving the memory of her husband in the past. One day she would marry again, but that day wasn't so close in mind. And I was still so fresh with the horror and the cruelty I'd suffered, that the embrace of a man wasn't something I was after. I knew - in time - that would change, and when it did I'd welcome it, but I felt no need to rush it along. Which left Robin as the only unanswered question for me.

Being handsome, pleasant, generous, I wondered why had he remained alone? I wished I could ask. I dared not. He was beyond all things an easy person to be with, but there was that way about him of command and a quiet reserve that said, without him saying it, "don't ask me certain things." So I didn't. But it pulled at me.

Many times we talked at length and laughed together and the ease of the moment more than once made me think I might ask, but I didn't. The closest I ever came to understanding it, came on its own, from his lips, unsolicited.

The conversation was such:

"Marion, are you tired of this yet?"

"Tired?"

"Yes, of this life. The forest."

"No, not at all."

"It's cold, damp, without much of a future."

"It has a great future."

"And what's that?"

"The constant promise of peace, freedom, great companionship. What else would you want."

"Maybe walls, a great room with a great ceiling, a party to fill the room and food cooked by a master."

"You find fault with Albert's cooking?"

A laugh from him, "No, not at all, if you remember not to call it cooking!"

"Yes, well...it's different."

"To say the least...and do you miss that?

"I eat well enough here."

"But simply."

"Yes."

"And, in your heart, are you a simple person, content with simple things...I think not."

"A few months ago I'd have agreed with you, but now.......well, things have changed."

"This place, the forest, it can do that to you. It can change you, or at least make you see things differently."

"Has that happened to you?"

"What?"

"Changed you. Made you see things differently?"

"Yes, I believe it has. I see a lot of things differently now."

"For instance?"

"My needs are different."

"In what way?"

"I came here on the run, full gallop as it were, literally. I thought it was necessary. I thought I needed to be here, not just for my own safety, but because there was no other place I could find the answers. I needed to find answers." He stopped and several minutes passed. I thought he might be waiting for me to say something so I did.

"What kind of answers?"

"Why I couldn't see it coming. Why I couldn't save my father. Why I couldn't save myself."

"And have you found those answers?"

"No." He looked away, then his eyes covered me in a very different way than any time before. It was the way any woman would like to be looked at. "Marion, you're very beautiful. It would be a shame for you to waste this beauty here." He waved an arm at the forest.

"But I love it here. For me, this is true beauty. And peace."

"It's beautiful, and most of the time it's peaceful. But it's still a damp, dark forest and your beauty belongs out there, in the light."

"Thank you. But I prefer it here, unless......."

"Unless what?"

"Unless you'd rather I not be here."

"Of course not. But you make a mistake."

"What mistake."

"Saying it's my decision. This isn't my forest."

"Oh yes it is. Very much yours. I don't believe there's ever been a forest that belongs more to one man than this one to you. You've made it your forest." He laughed, shook his head no. "It is. This is your forest. They can call it Sherwood Forest, but it's really Robin Hood's forest!" He laughed again, and put an arm around my shoulder.

"It's true I've called it mine. But there's those who'd disagree. And they'd be right. If anything is true, it's that I've usurped this place, in defiance of the laws of England."

"If you have, it's never been put to better use." He dropped his arm and looked at me again, in that same way as before and I knew that we had become, in a very short time, the very best of friends. Then there was an embarrassed distance in his eyes. An uncertainty. I wanted to reassure him that I had not taken any offense to his arm around me. But I said nothing.

****

The great battle, we all called it that, was something I still believe wasn't truly wanted by anyone, but was thought to be – in some indefinable way – necessary. I dreaded it and I know many others did also, but once decided on, there was no hesitation in the hearts of anyone. It was, in looking back, then that the winds began to turn a darker side toward us and blow a less friendly breeze – sometimes I think it was the forest deciding to exhale us back to where we had come from – telling us we couldn't solve our problems by hiding from them. Sometimes I believe it wasn't this, but rather our subconscious choice to find a way to drive ourselves back into the very world we had run from – each for their own private reason. Whatever it was, even if it was nothing, there was, for me, a change in the sound of the forest from that time forward.

When they trampled back into camp it was obvious what had happened, they had won, but at what cost? Never had a man been lost in raiding travelers on the winding paths of Sherwood, and never had those petty raids done anything to rouse great anger against us. Certainly they annoyed and pricked at those who were stopped and relieved of their purse, but their complaints, for the most part fell on deaf ears. The Sheriff was too fat and comfortable to care very much, and Prince John was busy with far greater troubles and also didn't care much for anyone losing anything so long as it wasn't his purse that was lost. And in truth, what was taken from the travelers was not enough to change the lifestyle of any of them. If truth be told, that portion that was carried to the poor wasn't enough to change their life style either. The part of the great legend of Robin Hood that tells of taking from the rich and giving to the poor was exaggerated because it was made to seem we changed the poor of England and we didn't. We gave them some intermittent, momentary joy, a little here, a little there – a better meal, new shoes or leggings – but the plight of the poor remained the plight of the poor. What we did perhaps do was make it seem possible something could be done, but done successfully only if it were attempted by a far greater force than our small band of forest renegades. If there was to be significant change to the life of the poor it would not, could not, come from a band of men in a forest stealing purses and giving out a portion of it. It had to come from the government, from the king and the nobles, from those with enough to make a difference. We were certainly not enough to make a difference. This isn't to say the legend should be any less than it is. We did stop the rich, relieve them of a token of their wealth, which was the symbol of their dominance, and then give some of that symbol to those who struggled under the yoke of poverty. That can't be denied. And it was a noble pursuit, a fine action on our part, but the wealthy were far too well entrenched, and the poor too far down the pole for us to make any kind of permanent and far reaching change. But, I believed then and still do, if we had continued along that tact, the safety of the clearing in the forest where we lived would have remained inviolable. It was the challenge to the Prince, it was that raid on the caravan outside the borders of Sherwood, that challenge to authority on a much larger scale, that brought about the retribution. And that was only the first of it because what then followed was a far more devastating scourge, from an unseen hand – a scourge that would eventually wipe the forest clean of us, leaving only the stories that would become legend. What I would have given to stop it!

****

The hunting of boar wasn't so unusual, though not nearly so common as deer. It was often more for sport than for the game. It was a difficult and dangerous creature and deer was much more plentiful. But, we had had an unusually tranquil period of weeks with few travelers to break the monotony, and a good stretch of fine weather. The men were restless. When they left that morning I thought very little of it other than that we would be eating boar, of which I wasn't particularly fond – it was neither as tender nor as tasty as venison.

When the men scrambled back into camp with Robin on the stretcher he was pale and there was a great stain of blood on his leg. When I learned exactly what had happened I became fearful. There was no secret about the terrors of a wound becoming infected. When the days passed and it finally came - you could see it, and if in doubt, the smell confirmed it – the agitation in the camp reached a peak. When it was decided that Parmon should be sought I asked Cally who he was. What she told me was bad and good. His reputation with herbs and potions boded well for his patients, but what she said about his equally rabid reputation for wild elixirs and promises of eternal youth made me wonder where lay the separation between what he was truly capable of and what he wasn't at all capable of. Pen, Tuck and Will left early and returned just after nightfall. Robin had deteriorated during the day and regardless of my concerns about this man called Parmon, I'd have been receptive to anyone who might be able to help. He was an ugly man, rail-thin and with the longest fingers I'd ever seen. They seemed to be constantly in motion, like a player on the lyre. He had a strange smell about him, not so much of the unclean as of smoke and sweet fragrances mingled in a fire. I was uncomfortable about him and didn't let my eyes stay very long in contact with his. Tuck treated him with utter contempt and it was clearly certain that if he wasn't successful in saving Robin's leg - or his life if it reached that point - Tuck would dispatch him in the blink of an eye. He went to work almost as soon as the hood was removed. He called for a fire to be made near Robin, and wanted two small pots. Everything he asked was done immediately. No one questioned his working, except Tuck who constantly demanded to know the how and why of what he was doing until Parmon summoned up the courage to tell him to "leave me alone!" At which point John took Tuck aside and they had long words. Aside from Robin, John was the only one who could manage Tuck when he was in one of his moods.

On the morning of the second day Robin woke and for the first time since the wound, sat up. His color was nearly back. Parmon hung quietly in the back, not paying much attention to us, rather he looked the camp, the trees and then moved in a great circle around the edges where the clearing met the forest. I wondered that he seemed so intent on it all and had such little interest in his triumph. By midday Robin had eaten twice and was in good spirits. The recovery seemed miraculous and my friend to whom I will give this manuscript, told me that whatever else was said of Parmon, it would always be said that he had saved the leg and probably the life of Robin Hood. I agreed, and for that reason he seemed a little less distasteful. By evening it was decided that Parmon would leave. He'd given two vials to John and said there was nothing more he need do. They blindfolded him and he was led from the camp.

Within two days Robin was on his feet and recovered. It was a fine time then and the camp was back again with good feelings. But I could see that Tuck was troubled and when I asked him he said "I don't trust that skunk." I asked had he not be blindfolded all the way in and out of the forest? "Yes. But that means nothing where someone like that's concerned." I asked if he meant that he believed in the stories of Parmon being a witch and capable of a witch's powers. "I don't know much about witch's or their supposed power. Maybe they can do things, maybe they can't. But I do believe in the evil of men like Parmon. I voiced against him before we brought him here. I knew it had to be done. But I hated doing it. And I feel the same way now." I wish Tuck had been wrong – but he wasn't.

We passed some comfortable months, the weather being good and the gold from the great battle being enough to sustain us for a great while. There was only one small intrusion in the calmness of the camp and it was something that we paid little attention to, but perhaps should have paid it greater heed. Illnesses crept in and out of camp. Small at first, just discomforts and the like, then deeper with some of the men becoming weak and pale for several days on end. It seemed to start not long after Harold brought Sean to us, and in fact it was Sean and Harold who seemed to suffer the most. Whatever it was, it came and went and always the men recovered and were themselves again, but it was like a wind that swept in and out, at will. Several of the men developed a hacking cough, but it too would come and go and we thought it was the food we ate or the dampness, although that had never affected us before.

When the sentinels rushed into the camp and declared that a large force of men had entered at the north end of Sherwood and were moving in a direction that would bring them directly to the camp in less than two hours Tuck jumped to his feet. His mouth opened and something reached his tongue but he stopped it. Robin asked questions of the sentinels then dispatched Gregory and several men, telling them that one should remain to scout them and the other to come back with new information. "You have to be back within an hour!" He said. "An hour! No more!" He told them exactly what he wanted them to look for and he was in every way the general he always was when we needed one. He gathered all of us around the great table and began to lay out his plans. His thinking was rapid and it amazed me to see him put together the defense so quickly and have it all before them in scarcely less than half an hour. Then they broke from the table and began to amass the weapons – bows and quivers no swords. His plan didn't call for swords, except for Tuck, Little John and five men of their choosing. He said he believed that it might be possible to bring the force to its knees without the loss of a single man. How? John had asked. How could that be? The archers had been deadly in the great battle and still the losses were heavy. "We'll draw them down man by man. You and Tuck and your men need to be ready as a diversion. But if I'm right, your swords will never see daylight."

The men left in a long line. Cally and I and Passy made our way to Marigold clearing. We would wait there until someone came to tell us to move back to the camp, or to go elsewhere – depending on what happened. It was two hours walk to Marigold and once there we passed the rest of the day waiting. It was just before dusk that we heard their voices and the trampling of their feet in the underbrush. When they broke from the woods there were smiles on every face. Pen told me how they had been positioned in the trees, higher than ever, at spots picked by Robin all along the trail from the campsite to the creek and how they had brought down so many of them and how Thoren had raged about and screamed at them to "come down and fight like men!" How Thoren had gone on to the camp and found it empty and after spending the night, set off again on the same trail and been waylaid again and eventually limped off into the clear land with Thoren the last man out, standing alone just at the edge of the forest, in the morning sun, bowing, just once. It was a great day. The last one we ever had in Sherwood.

I cared little about where the arrow came from, or who shot it. The man named Potelle may well have been the archer. In fact he probably was – there was little reason to doubt what Tuck had said. But in the end I cared only that it struck Robin and in so doing it struck us all. When he went down there wasn't a sound, you could have heard an ant on the leaves. My heart went out of me and it never completely returned. It was like the day Prince John had come into my rooms, only worse. It was a rape that was deeper and more vile than anything the Prince could have done to me. I said it so no one could hear me, "It's over now, live or die, it's over."

It was a sad day when we left. John, myself, Tuck and Pen to travel to the monastery, and Cally to Shockwell. I was distressed at having to say goodbye to Cally and felt worse that I'd found it necessary to lie to her when I told her I'd see her again in the spring at Marigold clearing. Not that I did not very much want to, but in my heart I didn't believe it would happen.

****

The monks at the monastery received us amiably. And soon I had Robin at ease in a small room with a strong fire. John stayed several days then said he was going to Martha and would be back by the middle of March. Will left the same day. Two days later Tuck and Pen left, saying they were going to Shockwell and would be back the following day. I thought nothing more of it than that, though Robin seemed uneasy. I asked him why he was out of sorts, was it the wound? He said no. What then? Nothing he said, nothing. I knew then that something was going to happen. I had my answer when Pen came back alone. He pulled me quickly out of my room and told me what had happened. I had no words. There was nothing for me to say. Tuck was gone, that seemed impossible. He was too much Tuck to be gone. Imagining the earth without him was impossible. He stalked it with too much of himself and carried it on his shoulders when it needed tending. He was the life blood of everything brave, and even growling and grumbling and sharpening that sword he was still lovable, loyal, fearless Tuck. Where do men like him go when they are gone? To what place? To that place the Vikings call Valhalla? I hoped so because there he would be tended to by the Valkyrie and it was no secret that Tuck loved the ladies. But, if there is no Valhalla, then what? I worried about that because I couldn't, didn't want to think of him wandering alone. As much as he preached solitude and his lack of need for anyone I knew, we all knew, it was just bravado. Tuck lived to be loved and loved everyone who lived with him. Pen asked if I thought Robin strong enough to be told. I said he must be told. He would never forgive us if we held this back. It was agreed quickly and we went to him. He said nothing for a long time. Then he asked Pen if it were certain Tuck was gone, which seemed strange because Pen had told him that he witnessed it. But Pen dutifully answered yes. "And you saw it yourself? You were there when it happened?" Again we looked at each other. Pen said yes again, and then Robin seemed finally resigned to it. And for the rest of the day he sat and stared at the walls of the room. He said nothing. Pen and I left him to himself until food was ready. At the table he said nothing until we had eaten, then he said, "He was a good man. I loved him as I would have loved a brother. But, it's done and we'll say nothing else about it. Ever." Then he asked if I would raise the fire. Two days later Pen left, promising to return in March and make the journey with us to Sherwood. It was now just Robin and myself and the winter. The winter of my saddest year.

Robin recovered to some extent – to that point where he had good days and bad days, but was never fully his former self. I saw it in his eyes, in his face which remained gaunt and chalky. And though I was no student of medicine or alchemy, I knew there was more to it than the arrow wound – which had healed completely.

A month passed and then the young woman, with the badly battered face came to the monastery with the note and the parcel. Pen had told us of the death of Parmon and what Tuck had done to Tuck, but he had never told us of the woman. And after learning of it I wondered why he had said nothing of it.

She handed the note to Robin, her hands were shaking so, I thought she would drop it. He opened it and read. Then he handed it to me. It was short and without excuse. It was the kind of note you destroy after you've read it so that you are sure that no one else will ever read it because you are sure that it was never meant for public eyes. After reading it I gave it back to Robin. He asked me to put it in the fire. I did so. We watched it burn. Then she gave him the parcel and by the time he'd opened the string she had risen and was at the door. He called her back. She turned, she was trembling again. I thought she would fall. "Marion, help her!" I put an arm around her and brought her to the stone bench opposite Robin. "Some wine." He said. I came back with it as quickly as I could. She was sitting quietly now, her face hung low, wiping her eyes with a handkerchief. She took the wine gratefully. Robin motioned to me. I went to him and he opened the leather sack. It was filled with gold coin. Having read the note he didn't have to tell me where it had come from, nor the reason it was here. He asked the girl that she tell him all she could about the death of Tuck. I wondered why he'd done so. Pen had given us all there could have been. I could only assume he was hoping for something else, something that might make the loss of Tuck less painful, or perhaps give it more meaning, more purpose. His request froze her at first, then she burst into a fit of crying. It was horribly intense and I thought she would shake herself to death. Nothing I did to console her helped. We waited. In time she calmed and then through interrupted speech she said she didn't know about the death of Tuck. The last she saw of him he was off toward the river. She assumed he'd gone back to the forest with his friend. Then she began to weep again. We waited. I regretted what she'd learned but perhaps it was best to have heard it from him. At some point she would have been made aware of it and it might have been done in a way that would have given her even greater pain. When she calmed again Robin asked her if she knew who he was. She said no. She'd just been told by Tuck to bring the note and the bag to the monastery and the monks would know what to do. She would have been here sooner, she said, but she had been recovering from her injury. He told her he was Robin Hood. She was surprised - and who did she think he was? A friend she said. Robin thanked her for being honest with the bag, it was a great deal of money. She said no thanks were necessary, and that she had thought Robin Hood to be dead - there were rumors in Edmonton that he'd been killed in a battle in the forest. He laughed and said he was quite alive. She managed a small smile. It seemed to twist her face and I saw it was painful. The scar across her cheek was ugly and long. It was a sad mark on a lovely face. He asked about the pain of her injury. She said it came and went. Then she looked squarely at him and said, "I know he was your great friend. I want you to know that I bear him no ill will." Robin said nothing. Then she said quietly, "I loved him, you know. I really did. I don't think he knew that. I hope he didn't. I'd have gone anywhere with him. I never told him that, but I would have. I loved him. Even after that night I still loved him and I forgave him and I'd still have gone with him. As a wife, or just a lover, even as a slave. I would have. Anywhere he would take me. I would have." I remember how I felt then, and how I feel now, recalling those words. They were said honestly, cleanly, without the slightest attempt to excuse anything or make us feel better or worse about her. They were said in a way that made me know she had to say them to someone, at least once. She had to say them aloud to someone so they would be known to more than just her and in doing so maybe Tuck would know, in Valhalla, or wherever, how much she loved him.

She said she must go. Robin thanked her again for fulfilling Tuck's final wishes and offered her gold from the bag. She said no, what Tuck had given her was far more than she deserved, far more than she would ever need. She asked him if she might kiss him. He asked why. "So that I might, if I ever have children, tell them I kissed Robin Hood." I wondered if the day would come when she would have children. She seemed so broken that I had doubts any man would ever put her back together again. Robin laughed and said yes. She gently kissed his cheek.

That night we sat before the fire. It was especially cold and I fed it large pieces of timber. It roared red and orange, and threw such heat that we were beyond comfortable. I was feeling melancholy. The visit by the young woman had left both of us with sad thoughts about the recent past. I remember clearly the conversation we had that night.

"It seems small and lonely."
"What does Marion?"
"The world."
"Why is that?"
"There's so few of us now."

"They'll return with the spring."

"Yes, I suppose."

"It's been a cold winter .

"Yes."

"But we're none the worse for it. Warmer here than in the forest."

"Yes, much more."

"It's the first winter in five years we're not together. I hope they all come back in the spring."

He was repeating himself, as he had come to do lately. "Of course they will."

"I hope so. John will see to it. He'll bring them back."

"It'll be fine again Robin, fine. Everyone will be back."

"It was cold and damp so often, but it was peaceful. And it was ours."

"Yes."

"It was all mostly good, I believe."

"It was all good."

"No, not all."

"I thought so. Except maybe the fighting. It would have been better if none of that had to be."

"Yes, the fighting was difficult. We lost friends to the fighting. There are times I wish we hadn't made the choice to fight. Maybe it could have been avoided. I wonder if I did enough? I wonder if I acted out of anger and made them do the same?"

"No, I don't think so. I don't think the choice was truly yours. You did what the time called for. You did what any leader does."

"I don't know. I used to believe that. I'm not so sure now. I look back and the truth is, it all started for the wrong reasons. Can something begun for the wrong reason be the right thing to do?"

"I don't understand."

"I could have tried harder. I could have fought her."

He was drifting between thoughts, something else that that was becoming more frequent. "Her?"

"Goneril. In the beginning, before the forest, I could have fought her. I could have demanded my life back. I could have made the right choices."

"Right choices?"

"Yes."

"You made the right choices. You always made the right choices because you always considered everyone before you considered yourself. Ask any of them! Ask me! I never saw you make a decision that wasn't made for the best of everyone."

"Maybe…but maybe not. I think too often we take the easy way."

"In all the time I've known you I've never seen you take the easy way."

"I did."

"And when was that?"

"When I decided you could make your own private world in the middle of everyone else's world. That was the easy way. And I made it worse when I decided that I knew what was best for other people. You can't do that. It's not fair to them."

"It wasn't your own private world and in the end it wasn't theirs either. It was nobody's private world. It was a place, in the middle of the world, where it was fair and just, all the time. Not just when it was convenient."

"It wasn't anything that glorious, Marion. It was just a little clearing in a big forest. A hideaway for misfits, and I was the biggest misfit. Nothing glorious in it, nothing grand. I thought it was, at first, but it wasn't. Just a hideaway. And you can't hideaway forever. The truth is, it served no purpose, changed nothing. What it did was give false hope."

"You'll feel differently in the spring."

"Do you really think they'll come back?"

"I'm sure they will." I had to lie.

"I'm not so sure."

"Why not?"

"We were young last fall. We're not young anymore. We've all become old men and women. I think Tuck knew that. I think that's why he left."

****

In early February he suffered a bout of illness. It lasted only four days, but it was discomforting because it had no basis in anything. One day he was fine, the next he was weak, tired and then down. When it passed he remarked that it was an aftermath from the wound. I agreed because it was easier to agree. But I saw in his eyes that he knew something was wrong, something inside, something that had really little to do with arrows. But since he didn't take it any further, neither did I. Before March arrived he had another attack of listlessness and fatigue. It came and went and we passed it off as before. As mid-March approached he became anxious. He walked the paths of the monastery straining his eyes for signs of John or Will or Pen. He wanted to be on the move. To leave for Sherwood. I cautioned him to be patient, we had to wait for the others. We would leave in plenty of time to reach Marigold clearing by the first of April. On the twelfth of March we were walking outside, in the fields, the monks were tilling the land. It was a particularly warm and fresh day, and Robin said it was a good omen for the upcoming year. He had been uncomfortable for several days, and it was obvious he was losing even more weight. His frame had dwindled to a shadow of what it had once been. He said he was in need of the forest. He wanted to believe it held some magical elixir that he had come to be dependent on. As we strolled we saw John approaching from the south. His arrival was a welcomed event and it put

Robin in the best spirits he'd enjoyed for some time. That night we sat before the fire drinking wine.

John announced that he and Martha were to be married. It made Robin very happy. He asked if John would bring her with him to Sherwood to live. John smiled and glanced at me. There was something uncomfortable in his look. I asked when it would take place and John said as soon as he returned. We agreed that we would accompany him to the cottage and be present at the wedding.

"We'll have a good time. Will and Pen, will be here tomorrow and then we can make for Shockwell. You'll be married with your friends for witness! And that'll make for a nice celebration before we go to Sherwood!" Robin was happy, bright. "To the wedding!" He raised his cup and we all drank. "Being away so long only makes me realize all the more how much I love that forest! And the way of life we live in it!" He was especially happy, and I found myself wishing we could go back and stay in Sherwood forever, with Robin happy, healthy and at peace with himself. But there was a truth in me that had a very different outlook, one I was trying to avoid. Robin talked again about how we would all travel together and how much he was looking forward to the wedding and then the return to Sherwood and the reunion with all the men. During all of it I saw John trying to smile, but it was poorly done. It was the first sign that he was holding back something and the more Robin spoke of it, the more he became uncomfortable. "The sheriff tried, Prince John tried, and they've lost. It's our forest, and we'll keep it as long as we like!" Suddenly he began to cough. I handed him a cloth. He wiped his mouth and gave it back. There was blood on it. I stuffed it quickly into the pocket of my dress. John looked at me, I shook my head. Robin asked, "So, tell me, John, what've you heard during the winter about Scarlett, Pen, and the others?"

John lowered his head. He held his tongue for what seemed an eternity. I knew what was coming next would not be good. But I knew whatever it was, he'd held it back for as long as he could. "Robin, Patrick is dead, and Martin is gravely ill, it's doubtful that he'll survive the month."

A moment of incredulous silence. Robin looking at John, then at me. "Dead? Patrick? Martin dying? Why? What happened?"

"Patrick became very weak, suddenly, without warning. Then he caught a chill, then he was dead, it was only a matter of five days."

"And Martin?"

"He complained of his stomach. You know he has always had problems with his bowels. It became worse. It was a month and a half ago. He moved between recovery and being sick as a dog. He seemed unable to fight it. He tried very hard. I went to see him last month. I didn't recognize him at first, he was so thin, so pale. He looked old. He died only a few days later."

"What was it?" He grabbed unconsciously at his own chest, then as if he'd done something he should not have, he pulled his hands away. "What was it John? What killed them?"

"I don't know." John bit down hard. I knew there must be more, but even in my wildest moment I would not have imagined what was next. "Robin, nine others are also gone."

"What do you mean gone?"

"Dead."

"What?"

"Dead Robin, and who isn't dead is ill, too ill to travel and certainly too ill to live in Sherwood. I've been to see some of them. Alan-a-dale is badly off. Albert can just about get around on a cane. I saw Gregory a fortnight ago, he was bedridden." It was the greatest silence I have ever heard and it shut out all the world. They say silence is the absence of sound but silence can be louder than sound. It can vibrate in your ear like a waterfall. It did so for me in that exact moment and ever since that night I have never felt that silence is golden, it can be the color of coal. "Robin, no one's coming back to Sherwood."

"I don't understand?"

"There's something that's taking them, one by one." Robin looked at each of us in turn. I knew he wanted to say something but couldn't find the words. John said what had to be said.

"It's over." I could see the pain it was causing him to be the bearer of such news, to have to say it so finally, but there was no choice. "The men love you, but they've had a bad winter. They're all weak, spent, ill with something no one understands. They sense the end. They love you, the forest, what you gave them, but it's beyond them now. They haven't a choice."

"Not a single man?"

"The only ones who aren't ill in some way are Pen, Cally, Marion, you and I." I was glad he'd included Robin, even though the lie was blatant. I was more than glad that Robin didn't question his name being a part of it. "I'm sorry to have to tell you this, Robin, but it's the truth. And there's no changing it."

"I don't understand how this can be. I've been here waiting for the spring. With all my heart I've prayed for spring!"

"Believe me, I wish it was different, but there's no changing it."

"How can this be?" He was incapable of fathoming it. Incapable of believing it. I felt helpless.

"Robin, the Bible says all things must pass. And Sherwood, has to pass. Has passed."

He rose and walked from us. John started after him, "John, no!" I whispered. He sat back. "Leave him to himself."

"How long has he looked like this?"

"A while. But more lately. You didn't name Tuck. You know about him?"

"Yes."

"Sad." I said

"Yes. I remember him every day. I loved that man!"

Several more minutes of silence.

"What now John? Where does Robin go?"

"The winter proves one thing at least. The Sheriff has little interest in Sherwood Forest. There's no price on anyone's head. Thoren left for France. Prince John has his own troubles. Robin is free to go where he chooses. Rumors have been running in the villages, even so far as London, that he's dead."

"And what will he do?"

"I have some money put aside, I can help."

"I don't mean money John. Tuck sent more than enough. I mean what will he do as a man? What will he become?"

John looked at me as if I had two heads. I saw it in his eyes and realized how much I'd been avoiding it. Avoiding it so much that I'd nearly convinced myself of it. "Marion," he said, "whatever it is that struck the others down, is striking him down. You must see that. You must see how he's changed, how he looks?"

"Yes."

"Then all that's left is to make him as comfortable as possible."

"Maybe he'll come through this. Maybe with the spring and…"

"And what? There's no forest, no men. Marion, there's no Robin Hood any more, at least not the Robin Hood he was. There's just the stories, the truths and the lies and the exaggerations, but there's no clearing filled with men, and there's no Robin Hood."

"I know." I hated saying it, but it was so very true.

"He can live at the monastery. If he chooses not to, he can live with me and Martha."

"He would never do either."

"He has no choice!" He rose and paced. I said nothing. "Would he stay with you?"

"Me? I don't know. Maybe he would. But where, here? I'm telling you he won't stay here. I'm afraid he's going to insist on going back to the forest."

"You can't let that happen! That's insane!"

"It's not easy to tell him what to do."

"He's been with you a long time now. He's fond of you. Maybe more than fond......."

"John!"

"He is Marion, he's fond of you. More than that I'll bet. He'll heed what you say."

"What he feels for me is friendship. I wish it were more, but it's not. I've given him so many chances to say it. It's just friendship, maybe a great friendship, but nothing more. And that friendship won't make him less than he is. He'll insist on the forest, I know he will."

"You have to keep him out of there. Whatever is left to him will be gone in a month if he goes back into Sherwood!"

"But he is Sherwood, and Sherwood's him!"

"Not anymore."

"That's cruel John!"

"No, it's the truth. Sherwood is a death sentence."

"He's already got a death sentence. What's the difference if he gets another one. You can't hang a man twice!"

"All right, it's not easy for you, but it's not easy for me either. Sleep on it. We can talk_ again tomorrow."

Later that night I sat with Robin in the antechamber between our rooms.

"It's very hard to believe."

"Yes."

"I don't mean that it's happening, I mean the suddenness of it. I knew it would have to happen some day. But I thought it would be a long time from now. And I thought it would be slow. A gradual parting, a bit at a time until it was gone. Some time to get used to it. But now, to happen so fast. In one swoop. To be over, just like that, without even a goodbye, not even a sad farewell. No gathering to shake hands, no embraces, no tears, no laughter, no talking of past glory, no promises to meet each year for old times sake. Nothing, just the cold hard end of death. Something about it's all wrong."

"We can go north. I've always wanted to go north. We can live free and without worry. No more battles, no more dead friends."

"I'd like to see the forest once more. Just once. The clearing, the camp, just once more. Then we can go north. We can go wherever you want to go. But I need to see it just once more."

"Why, what for? What purpose can it serve?"

"I need to say goodbye to it. I'll never be happy leaving this world if I don't say goodbye to Sherwood."

The next morning John and I talked. We agreed that after the wedding I'd take Robin to Sherwood for a few days. "Then you have to make him live up to his word and go north with you. Agreed?"

Will arrived in the afternoon. He didn't look good. Robin said nothing about it, greeting him as if nothing were wrong. He was carrying a note from Pen. Robin read it, laughed and tossed it into the fire. He never spoke of what it said. I never asked, but I knew it meant that Pen wouldn't be coming. The following day John and Scarlett left. Robin and I would follow in two days.

****

We made our way to the wedding in a cart drawn by a single horse. I knew that John and Martha would journey to Cheshire after the wedding where Martha's brother was a vassal to Lord Breckinridge of Tourney. There John would pledge his fealty and farm his portion of the land. There he and Martha would begin their family. Robin and I talked of that and he seemed very pleased John had found peace. He kept telling me that having considered it, he was glad it was over, all of it, the forest and the cold and the damp and the fighting. I didn't really believe him, and I was sure he didn't believe it either. But it was better than having him pine for it. Perhaps if he lied to himself long enough and hard enough he'd actually begin to believe the lie and then it could become a memory, maybe even a good one.

It was a long day. I was concerned the trip would bring on another attack. I had suggested that we make two days of it, but he'd insisted he was fine and we would continue. As we came up on the cottage John came across the field to us.

"Where's Martha?" Robin asked."

"Inside, preparing for tomorrow. Passy's on his way, and Archie too! They're both feeling better and should be here tomorrow, early morning!"

"That's good news."

"Here she comes." Martha was moving through the field.

In the evening, after dinner, we sat in the cottage before the fire. The first breath of summer although it warmed the day, wasn't strong enough to hold onto the nights.

Perhaps it was the ale, perhaps it was the pain, perhaps it was something unknown that makes men speak in ways that seem akin to fancy.

"John, I've formed a new band." Robin said suddenly.

John looked at me, then at Martha. Passey was about to speak but Archie shook his head. Then everyone looked at me. I had little help to offer except to say, "Robin, you can't be serious?"

"I am."

"Why?"

"There's still work to be done."

"What work?"

"The work we started, the work we haven't finished. And I'll finish it, so long as I can draw a bow, I'll finish it." He stopped suddenly and then he was gone, his eyes glazed over and he was somewhere else. John looked at me and I tried to tell him without words that I'd seen this before, the sudden shifts of mood, the sudden obtuse, senseless rambling. Then Robin came back, his voice low and muffled as if he were talking to us and not talking to us, talking to someone in his head. "I've found seven men, young, strong, good with the bow, one an expert with the sword. They're meeting me in Sherwood. We'll move out after the wedding. They have friends who'll join us in the fall, after the harvesting is done."

Robin continued to speak of what he would do, talking of the glory of it all. John and I and the others sat quietly obedient to his rambling. Agreeing with his enthusiasm and hoping it would end soon because every word made it more painful to endure. I felt a screaming in my head that made my vision blur. And still he continued, as if he were going to go on forever in a rambling, wondering fairyland of dreams and wishes and hopes that were as far from reality as anything I had ever seen. He wasn't even remotely aware of the surroundings and the people, and occasionally he spoke to Tuck as if he were standing right in front of him. Then he rambled about the past, the why and the wherefore of it.

"I was alone that day I first went into Sherwood. But then there was Pen, and everything changed. It grew and grew until we were an army. What great days then, what great days to come! You know John, we're going to do more. Not sit around a campfire and waste away the years. No. We're going to bring them in by the hundreds and then when we're ready we'll move out against Prince John. We'll storm the castle, we'll take it and it'll be our base. From there we can......." He was suddenly silent. I saw that all strength had gone out of him. He began to cough, a hacking, brutal cough. I placed a cloth over his mouth. Everyone rose slowly and went outside. I laid him on a blanket on the floor of the cottage. When he was asleep. I joined the others.

"Marion, he's so very ill. Even more than just a few days ago!"

"He has ups and downs, John. Some days he's fine and then not so good."

"He's bones Marion, just bones."

"I know. But no matter what you do there's no controlling it."

"And this craziness about starting again! It would be insane even if he were healthy. It's over Marion."

"Don't you think I know that?"

****

Two days passed at the cottage.

Two miserable days.

Then we left. I'd convinced Robin that he needed to rest for awhile before making the journey to Sherwood which was a full three days. He agreed, reluctantly. We went northeast to the village of Umberton in Lincolnshire. It was only a day from where John and Martha would be. We settled into a small cottage. No one knew who he was. And that was good. Often when I went to the village I heard his name spoken. I heard people say he was dead. Killed by knights of the sheriff of Nottingham. His band of outlaws dead, or scattered. I told him about each new story and he smiled at every one. I thought the smiles weren't real, but it was long past the time when anything could be done about that.

All in all I'd be lying if I said it wasn't a difficult time. Actually there were days when it was horrible – but then there were those days, sometimes several in a row, when it was very good and he seemed almost the old Robin, thinner, pale, but at least in good spirits. But I never allowed myself to believe it would ever again be anything constant, always knowing it would eventually become a horror - and I lived in fear of what I'd do then. How I would remain strong enough. How I would help him face it. In the meantime, each time he fell low, I worked with all my heart to bring him back, but even when it seemed I was successful, he wasn't the same as he had been days before. With each new bout he lost a little of himself. It ravaged him cruelly. A man who had always regarded sleep an unnecessary inconvenience lay sleeping in the bright light of day. The sight of him, so old before his time, so helpless, brought me down so low. I tried not to let it show. I don't know if I was successful. Fingers that had once drawn a bowstring better than any man in England, could no longer hold a quill still enough for writing. He'd begun a diary, but gave it up. There was a short period of respite. It came with the first day of June and although I was grateful for it, I was also afraid it would bring back the desire to see Sherwood one more time. I'd avoided any mention of woods and forests in the hope that he'd forgotten about my promise to take him there. He hadn't, and several days of feeling better than normal brought with it what I dreaded.

"Marion, it's time to go."

"Go where?"

"To Sherwood."

"I think we should wait Robin."

"Wait for what?"

"For August, when it's warm."

"It's July, it's warm now."

"But August is the best month in the woods. You know that."

"It doesn't matter. July is fine enough."

I tried to dissuade him the rest of the day, but he would have none of it. I had promised him, and feeling better made him all the more insistent. I had no choice and thought I might as well get it over with. My thinking was that once done and back in the cottage, it would be finished and then we could settle into whatever time remained and I could do all that was possible to see to his comfort. Which seemed all that was left to me.

When the day came to begin he was in good spirits and anxious to go.

"Marion, the day's broken!"

"I'm nearly ready!"

The first day, after traveling only five miles, Robin, insisted on stopping at an inn for some ale early in the afternoon. At sunset we were still there, drinking ale and laughing. I suggested we take a room and spend the night. He agreed and I was grateful.

While Robin slept I lay in my bed and for the first time since that rush from the castle I allowed myself to consider it fully – and to take the liberty to conjure up a fantasy – to wonder what might have been had we been able to love each other, or rather had he been able to love me, because there was no doubt in my mind that I loved him. It seemed unfair that I should have found a man I could have spent the rest of my life with - even if it was only as a companion – and he was being taken from me before we had hardly begun. I was angry at the world and everyone in it. It seemed to me I'd been cast a bad lot from the very beginning, or at least since that day when I left France for England and a life at court. I was suddenly, and for the first time, angry at my father for having sent me. He had believed it to be in my best interests, but it had turned out very badly. The Prince, the man who was supposed to be my guardian, became my enemy, and the country that was supposed to be my second home was far from that. It had all gone awry, wild with mistakes and misfortune. And even now, with so much having passed beneath my feet, there was little I had dreamt of that had any chance of becoming reality. I felt very sorry for Robin and very sorry for myself.

In the morning we breakfasted and took to the wagon. We had been told there was an inn ten miles along the road. It was a longer distance than I'd planned but the day promised to become warm once the fog burned off and Robin seemed bright and a little stronger, so I set out with a lighter heart.

Half an hour from the inn, we were moving along a high road several feet above the fields which were spread out on either side. The morning mist was unusually thick, unusually gray, the color of burning weeds. It hung heavy and damply. It was difficult to see very far ahead.

Suddenly we heard the rustling sound of footsteps, coming out of the fields, very close to the road. I strained my eyes, the road was narrow, the slope on either side very steep, and I didn't want to run the cart off the level. Then the steps seemed very close and I pulled up the horse. Three men were suddenly in front of us. They seemed to have burst without warning through the fog. As they approached the tallest of them, a lanky man, spoke out, "Hey there!" The other two were a step behind him and there was an air about him that he was the leader of the group. "How are you today?"

"Fine." I said, straining to make out their faces. They continued to approach and when they were only several feet distant, the tall one pulled out a sword and the other two, a short stocky man heavily bearded with long matted hair, and a younger, almost boyish lad with light brown hair hanging in ringlets beneath a cap, and torn leggings, pulled out daggers.

"We'll take your money if you please!" said the tall one. At first I thought it was a joke because he was smiling and the sound of his voice had pleasant lilt.

"No harm to you." said the stocky one, "Just give us the money and be on your way."

Now I knew it wasn't a joke. They obviously meant to rob us, but what else? A year ago I would have felt sympathy for them, knowing that they were about to be taught a lesson. But now, it was the opposite. Robin, who had sat perfectly still, said quietly, "Bandits."

"Did I hear you say bandits?" the tall one shouted.

"That's what I said."

"We're not bandits, we're outlaws."

"Either way, outlaws or bandits, the same thing."

"Oh no, very different, very different. Don't you know the difference?"

Robin shrugged. The tall lanky one with the sword seemed suddenly affronted, as if the use of the word bandit was offensive to him, but outlaw wasn't. That he should be making a distinction of it seemed insane. He told us to get out of the cart. I didn't know what to do. Robin nudged me and I did as they said. We stood beside the cart as the tall one paced in front of us several times, swaggering and moving his sword in an arc in the air, threateningly, warning us that we should give him no trouble. "Hey boys, look, he has a sword!" He pointed to the sword Robin carried. "I wonder, can such a wasted thing even pick it from the scabbard! Perhaps we should run before he decides to hurt us!" All three laughed. In the deepest part of my heart I wished for the past, and what might have been.

"Put down that sword before you hurt yourself." Robin said. I wrapped my arm in his and tugged at him. He ignored me. It seemed a bad time for him to become argumentative. Perhaps it was best just to give them the money and hope it was all they wanted.

"Arrogant fool isn't he," said the young one with a voice that confirmed he'd not left childhood very long ago. Then he backed up a few paces, and disappeared into the fog.

"Watch your tongue young man." Said Robin.

"Oh, oh, the skinny fellow has a bite!" The tall, lanky one said as he came close to Robin. The others joined him in laughing - the laughter of the young one coming from out of the fog. "Give me the money, and I'll forget the insult," the leader said angrily. "Give me the money and I'll let you go!"

"I'll give you nothing."

"Nothing, did you say? Nothing was it?" The tall one chucked and seemed to be enjoying what to him was apparently great fun. He turned to his two comrades, of which only the stocky one was visible, the young man not having come back out of the fog. "Nothing he says! He calls us bandits, then says he'll give us nothing. Doesn't know the difference between bandits and outlaws. Stupid man, probably doesn't know how to read or write. I'm sure of it. Doesn't know how to read or write! Of course not, so that's why he doesn't know the difference. Well, maybe we should talk to the lady about it! Maybe she knows. Maybe she can read and write. She's pretty enough, looks fine enough. She must be able to read and write and know the difference. She must know a lot more than the skinny one!" He shouted the last words and whirled at Robin, raising his sword above his head.

Robin stood firm. I held to his arm and breathed deeply. Something inside me suddenly said that if this were to be the time then so be it. If we are to go now, at least it's together, on the same day. Then the tall one came close to me and took up strands of my hair in his fingers.

"Don't touch her." Robin shouted.

"Oh! You hear him! Now he's giving orders." Shouted the stocky one, who laughed, and moved back into the fog, disappearing like the young one had.

"Well, he probably doesn't know who we are, so he feels a little brave. Do you know who we are skinny man? Do you?" The tall one had dropped my hair from his fingers and put his face so close to Robin that their noses nearly touched.

"Yes, I know who you are, you're thieves."

"Now it's thieves, boys. Now he calls us thieves! Yes, thieves. Thieves. Poor men. Which is why we take from the rich and give to the poor. We give to ourselves!"

"We're not rich."

"Well, we'll see about that after we take your purse. If it's empty we'll give it back. If it's not, then you're richer than we are and we'll take it! We'll take it like Robin Hood used to do. Like Robin Hood before they cut him up!" The tall, lanky man backed away, lowered his sword and, laughing, he moved into the fog, and then all three of them were gone from sight. Suddenly there was silence. I shuddered, and hoped. Perhaps they were gone. Of course that couldn't be true. Much as it seemed it was, this wasn't a game. Robin stroked my hand as I tightened my grip on his arm.

Suddenly the tall, lanky one jumped from the fog, like a clown jumping onto a stage from the pit of the orchestra, a grotesque expression on his face.

"Robin Hood, Robin Hood, and his merry men!" He sang like a minstrel performing at a show, all the while hopping about in front of us, brandishing his sword and grinning. "But all dead now, the sheriff's men killed him, killed him and his merry band! And we have taken to the roads and take the purses to our hearts in honor of Robin Hood!"

"Yes! The purse, if you please!" the voice of the youngest laughed from behind the curtain of the fog. The tall man whirled around and stood facing Robin with a sadistic smile. There was a pause and a moment of silence, then the short, stocky one came out of the fog with a slow, rambling gate, grinning like a clown. He moved toward Robin. As he stood opposite me I could smell him, old sweat mixed with the mist. A heavy, ugly smell.

"Hey, look at the lady!" he said putting his face so close to mine that I could feel his breath, "quite a comely little thing!" He reached out and touched the cuff of my dress. Robin struck down his hand and he laughed. "Oh, a brave knight!" Then he spun quickly on his toes whirling around several times like a top, and I wondered at the agility of one who was so thick and poorly put together. He stopped and tip toed, backwards, into the fog.

The tall lanky one said, "Well Peck, seems you have an eye for the ladies!"

"Always have!" Came the voice from the fog.

"Come here lassie, let me have another look at you. Perhaps we'll take you instead of money. We could use a little lady in our act. The Traveling Triumvirate has never had a lady as a member of their company. What say you to that Jocko?"

"We don't need a lady, they're more trouble than they're worth!" The voice of the young boy came from behind the curtain of the mist.

"Well," drawled the tall lanky man, "you'll change that tune when you get older! When you get older, when you get older!" He began to sing again, and the grotesque grinning reappeared on his face. He stopped singing and looked carefully at me. "It's been hard times for us these past months. Very hard. Our countrymen have forgotten what it means to pay to see the Traveling Triumvirate!"

"You're actors?" I blurted it out, couldn't help myself because suddenly I saw it - a performance, a horrid, frightening dance, a performance destined for an unhappy ending.

"Yes, actors. Or rather we were! There was a time, not long ago mind you, when we were counting the coins from our talent. Not long ago we traveled and sang and danced and gave the poems to the people and they paid well for our efforts. Now, the fat Prince makes the taxes, and the people have nothing for us. So, we make the road our stage and take the coins that would have been given freely!" The tall lanky man became serious and darkly angry, he craned his neck and his eyes closed to small slits. "See what we have to do to eat?"

"What does that have to do with us?" Robin said.

"Everything! Everything because you're here, on our road, our stage!" He made a low bow, leaning on his sword. Then he came close to me again, I could feel his breath against my cheek again. "You're very pretty! Very pretty!" He looked me up and down. "Are you friendly? Let me see how friendly you are!"

"See how friendly she is and let us watch!" The voice of the stocky man poured out of the fog.

"Marion. Don't move." said Robin firmly.

"I'm tired of his mouth Garvin, let me kill him." The young voice said as he emerged from the fog and took several steps toward Robin whirling his dagger in the air.

"If there's to be any killing I'll take the pleasure Jocko."

"No, wait, before you start the killing let me take her to the side of the road and tell you if she's a friendly lady! If she is, spare the skinny one!" The stocky man jumped from behind the gray curtain.

"Go to it Peck, go to it! Take her and find out if she's a friendly lady. If she is, then I'll have at her and when she's warm and a little tired, we'll let the boy have his time!"

Suddenly it was there, clear and pure, as it had once been. He pulled his sword from the sheath, it flew out with the speed of long gone days, with the power of that awful sound of steel on leather and death tugging at the blade. The tall man, still leaning on his sword didn't seem to believe what he was seeing, and he began to laugh, but his laugh was cut short as he was struck across the chest, right side to left, deeply, and it was done. He fell to the earth, his body quivered for a moment, then it lay still. The stocky one drew back in fear. The young one, spurred into action as if he were acting a part in a play - but a part previously unknown, something not memorized and not real, not motivated by a cue, not by malice or the knowledge of what he was doing - lunged forward with his dagger and plunged it into Robin, it made a horrible thump, then a sucking sound as he drew it out. He stared at it in his hand, then dropped it and recoiled from the horror of his own deed. I screamed! The stocky man looked at the two men, one dead, one stabbed and bleeding, turned and began to run down the slope and off the road into the still fogged fields with the sun just beginning to cut through the fog. The young one looked at the man he'd struck and seemed confused, as if the part he had just played had not been written for him, but for someone else and was one he was sorry he had played. He shouted something that sounded like lines from a poem about the enemy and the vindication of good against evil. Robin raised the sword again and I knew the boy would be dead. Dead long before he was ever old enough to know why he'd done what he had done, long before he would ever have the time to repent it. I shouted, "No! Don't kill him Robin!" I raised my arm to grab at his and he looked at me with the old fire in his eyes and for just a moment, just a second or two or three, I saw him live again as he'd once lived and because of that, because of who he was, who he'd been, who he still is, he lowered the sword. The boy, who had cringed into a small embryonic bundle peeked out from behind the arms that covered his face and said

very quietly, "Robin? Robin? Robin's dead!"
Then suddenly he shouted "You're no Robin,
you're a skinny old man that's killed my father!"
He spit at Robin and whirled around, racing into
the mist. Robin fell suddenly to one knee, turned
to his left and dropped onto the road. I covered
his body with mine. Some time passed. I don't
know how long. Perhaps a quarter hour. Then I
saw a form coming toward us. In fear I reached
for the dagger that lay on the ground, determined
to kill anyone who might move against us. It was
a worker from the field who had seen something
strange on the road as the fog lifted and had come
to investigate.

****

The following day when Little John
stormed into the cottage he frightened the farmer
and his wife.

"I'm his friend," he pointed to Robin,
who lay on the bed, "and hers," he nodded at me.
"I'm the one your son was sent to fetch."

The farmer looked at John, heard his
words, and turned to his wife. She was knitting
and didn't look up. The farmer rubbed his chin,
looking curiously at John, who turned to Robin,
unconscious, breathing with difficultly, hacking
sounds coming from his lungs,

"Marion, what happened?"

"Oh John!"

The farmer eyes had become wide.

"What is it you said? What did you call her?

John said nothing in response. He picked Robin up in huge, gentle arms and carried him outside to the cart, and we drove off with the farmer shouting after us,

"What did you call her? Who is he. Who are you?

****

After a time the horse lathered and we stopped to rest him. When we began again John walked beside the cart and we pushed the horse hard to make his cottage as quickly as possible. At the cottage it was two days of agony, during which Robin vacillated between life and death. On the morning of the third day as he lay sleeping I asked it.

"John, we have to take him to Sherwood."

"Sherwood?"

"Yes."

"You mean now?"

"Yes."

"For what reason?"

"It has to be. I promised him. I won't break it."

"Marion, the journey will kill him."

"Does that matter? He won't survive this cottage, so why not try and take him?"

He didn't answer. He paced.

"Does this have to be? Isn't it better that he stay here. Why put him through anymore pain?"

"It must be. It's what Robin wants. He has to die in Sherwood Forest, where he belongs. He has to die where he was really born. Where he became what he is, in the forest he made his, will always be his.......centuries are going to pass, centuries. Millions and millions of lives come and go. But Robin's eternal, and he's made his forest eternal. He has to die there, in its arms."

****

And this is exactly how it ended:

We were alone, the clearing was empty. It was cruelly void and abandoned. Forest grass had begun to pepper the brown earth – no feet to beat it down. The lean-to's had all but crumbled and where the great fire had been was only a black pile of dust. The King's Building was tilting, no one was there to prop it up, to make it right again. I felt a horrible sense of loss. Up to this point in my life it had been the best place I had known. Home. Laughter. Some sadness, some pain, and the seeing of death up close and very personal, but still, all considered and taken honestly, it had been the best place I had ever been and without doubt a place I could have lived forever. Now it was nothing, just another dark and empty clearing. No glory, no laughter and certainly no longer a refuge. It made me angry to see it that way and I hoped, demanded really, that there would be tales told by grandfathers to sons, by fathers to sons, and strangers to strangers. Tales that would keep alive the story of what had been there. Robin, John, Tuck, Pen, Cally, Will, all of them, each of them, had earned it, deserved it, I was sure of that.

"Please John, leave us. It'll be all right now."

"Are you sure Marion? I'll stay if you like."

"No John, I'd like us to be alone together...does that make you angry with me?"

"Angry? Why angry. You're his closest."

Little John left me with Robin, who lay asleep on the cool grass, in the early morning, with the sun just rising above the horizon, and a deer grazing not fifty yards away, peacefully and without fear. He'd once told me about the deer that had saved his life and I wondered if it had returned to say goodbye.

I sat beside the thin white form of what was once one of the most glorious men in England and did not know how to feel, what to be, what to do. But I knew God was in the forest, listening. I turned my eyes to the branches that covered me and asked him "Please, please, give him the strength to end with peace, this life that has given him such great suffering."

There was no reason to hold back the tears and it was best that they fall now, before he woke and I had to say goodbye. So while he slept I drained all that was inside, all that had been and all that would come after. And with the moments of silence granted to me by my Creator I made my peace with the forest and the man who crowned it and when the tears were over I wiped my eyes, told myself that he'd lived as he believed he should live. Had done what he believed needed doing. Never giving quarter to what he couldn't feel in his heart of hearts, never for a moment fearing the evil of man. And having lived that way, what could dying mean? What could it take away from him? It was just a temporary thing that would come along then be gone and then he would be Robin Hood again.

It was cool. The way it had been when it had been what it was. Cool and damp and the air was heavy with wet and the trees seemed like old friends who wanted to help. Have you ever been in a place in that way? Where it is what it had been and can really never be anything else, no matter what people do to it, or say about it. Have you ever been in a place when time stood perfectly still and you knew that if you had the secret you could make it stay that way forever?

"Marion?" His voice was very weak. He had opened his eyes and was smiling.

"Yes Robin, I'm here."

"You brought me back to Sherwood."

"Yes."

"Thank you."

"How do you feel?"

"Like any man feels who's reached the end."

"Stop it Robin, this isn't the end!"

"Nonsense lady," his voice, for a moment, had the old power, "it's a fine day, and the finer the day, the finer the death. I only wish it could have happened in a battle."

"You've fought enough battles."

"Maybe." I saw the anxiety come over him. "Marion, my grave has to be our secret. Will you promise me that?"

"Yes, I promise."

"Just you and Little John need know."

"Yes."

"What a day! How I love this forest, even the cold dampness of it. Even the wet clothes in the morning, the chill in your bones, I even love the occasional hating of it. I wish I had the time to spend more days, here, with you. Thirty-one seems so early to leave. It is, isn't it Marion?"

"Yes Robin, it's very early. Not even summer in the life of most men. Barely just the ending of spring. But then most men never do, in all the seasons of their life, what you have done in the very few seasons given to you." He drifted away again. I waited and I became angry and asked myself why? Why should his calendar be so much shorter than most?

"If I could I'd bend a knee to you! And to the men of Sherwood! But to the world Marion, to the world that's paid me little but grief, to the world I wouldn't bend a knee, say a thank you, or ask forgiveness! To the world I say I've done what I've done, and been the best I could. And I make no apology." Then came, the ugly, hacking coughing. When it stopped I asked,

"Robin, what should I do with the bow?"

"My father gave it to me. I should take it with me."

"Whatever you wish."

"You know Marion, I never feared death. I always believed it was a path to another place, or a path back here again. Either way is fine. But now that I face it, long before I ever believed I'd have to, I'm angry, because it's so soon, and there was so much more I could have done."

"Robin, please, let's not talk anymore about death today."

"Marion?"

"Yes."

"I'm thirsty." I reached for the skin and he drank while I held it for him.

I loved him so! Even now I do, with every part of my being.

"Marion, remember our night together?" His eyes lit for a moment and his voice changed. It was soft again, maybe a little melancholy and distant, as if he were somewhere else, not lying on the forest floor. He asked it again. I wasn't sure what night he meant. But I said yes. "Remember how we laughed. How we joked about it the next day? Remember what I said, what was all the fuss about?" He laughed, it brought him to a convulsive coughing. I pulled a cloth from my pocket. He tried to clear his throat, he gurgled with the effort. It was a sickening sound, and it threw his body up and down. When the coughing was over I wiped his lips, and pushed the cloth into the bed of leaves that surrounded us.

"Are you all right Robin?"

"Yes. Yes. It seemed so funny, remembering it now. So funny. But it wasn't funny at all. It was grand and I'd do it again if I could...would you? Would you do it again?" I nodded, though I still didn't know what night he was talking about, or what it was we had done that he felt so good about. Maybe it was a night that might have been, or one he'd imagined. "So much, so many things, would have been better if it could have been different for us."

"Must we talk about it now?"

"If not now, then when? I have very little time."

"That's not true!"

"Oh yes it is. We both know that. I'll not last the day. And that's fine. I've no desire left in me to last the day, even the hour. I'm tired Marion, tired of the victories and the defeats. Tired of being for everyone when I didn't have the strength to be for myself."

"You should rest, Robin."

"Why?"

"Please Robin."

His face became suddenly stiff, and his eyes wide and very open.

"Marion, I feel strange."

"What is it?"

"I don't know, I feel strange, as if everything is very far away. As if you're far away. Are you far away?"

"No Robin. I'm here."

"I can see you now. I can see you! Riding out onto the bridge over the moat! Riding to meet me! I see you now. I was afraid you'd left me! But you're here! Marion, we should have grown old together and died in each others arms when we'd had enough of this world."

I held tightly to his hands.

"Look Marion, they've come for us. They've come to take us back to Sherwood!"

"Who's come for us?"

"Look Marion, the sky is filled with angels!"

Proof

Made in the USA
Charleston, SC
04 May 2010